Acts of Contrition

Thomas Cobb

Texas Review Press
Huntsville, Texas

FIRST EDITION, 2003

Requests for permission to reproduce material from this work should be
sent to:

Permissions
Texas Review Press
English Department
Sam Houston State University
Huntsville, TX 77341-2146

Cover image: *Proverbium* **(Skeletal) by Stephen Fisher**
Photo of Thomas Cobb by Paola Ferrario
Cover design by Paul Ruffin

Library of Congress Cataloging-in-Publication Data

Cobb, Thomas, 1947-
  Acts of contrition / Thomas Cobb.-- 1st ed.
    p. cm.
  ISBN 1-881515-59-1 (alk. paper)
  1. United States--Social life and customs--Fiction. 2. Historical
fiction, American. I. Title.
  PS3603.O226 A64 2003
  813'.6--dc21
                                        2003008909

To Randy

Table of Contents

A Cold, Cotton Shirt

They were driving back from work, the three of them. They were driving the hundred miles from the mine at Superior where they worked during the week, to Tucson, where they all lived. In Tucson, they had families and homes, in Superior the three of them lived in a small trailer. Whitey, the oldest of them, liked to say, "There isn't a damned thing Superior about it."

They were about halfway home, talking quietly as the last light of that summer Friday afternoon failed. They passed a bottle back and forth and worked at putting the week behind them. Tony, the youngest, was nearly asleep in the back seat, lulled by the combination of rum, the long day they had just worked and the low murmur of the other men's voices. He tried to sleep. He wanted to be home in Tucson. He wanted to be with Eleanor, his girlfriend.

Sam was the one who saw it and told Whitey to stop. By the time Whitey got the car stopped, put into reverse and back the two or three hundred yards they had gone, Tony was awake. "What?" he asked. "What is it?"

"Jesus," Sam said. "It looks bad. Real bad."

"What?" Tony asked. "What looks so bad?"

What looked so bad was another car. It was in an arroyo at the side of the road, upside down. "Ouch," Whitey said.

When they got out, it seemed to Tony that the other car must have been there forever. It seemed too still, too settled into the arroyo to have ever been just another car driving down the deserted road behind them. Even the smell of gas and oil, which was still faintly in the air, seemed old and a part of this arroyo.

"Jesus," Sam said. "Would you look at this."

Tony and Whitey came around to the side of the car where Sam was crouched by the window. When they crouched beside Sam they saw the driver, suspended, pinned by the impact, hanging upside down.

"Is he dead?" Tony asked.

"What do you think?" Whitey asked Tony and Sam and maybe nobody.

Nobody answered, and Whitey reached his hand in through the window toward the pinned driver.

"Maybe you shouldn't do that," Sam said. "You're not supposed to move people who've had accidents."

Whitey couldn't quite reach the driver, so he got on his knees and crawled another foot, reaching in to the driver. He backed up, then sat up on his haunches. "Dead," he said. "He's dead."

"Maybe you don't know that," Tony said. "Sometimes people seem dead, only they're not."

"No," Whitey said. "He's dead. It smells like a still inside there."

Our car smells like a still inside, Tony thought.

"Well, we're going to have to get someone," Sam said.

"There's the bar, back where we were," Tony said.

"We'll drive back there and call the Highway Patrol," Whitey said.

As they walked back to the car, Whitey told them to wait. "Someone has to stay here," he said.

"He's dead," Sam said. "It doesn't make any difference. He won't get any deader alone."

"You can't leave a body alone. It's not right. There are coyotes. Robbers."

"Robbers? Here?"

"You can't leave a body alone. It's not right."

"I'm not staying," Sam said. "You stay then."

"I'm driving," Whitey said. Then, "Oh, hell. Let's draw straws. Short straw stays. He broke off three bits of dry weed and put them in his hand. Then he held them out to Tony and to Sam.

Of course, Tony thought when he got the short straw. Of course.

"The bar's about ten miles back," Whitey said. "We'll drive there, call the Highway Patrol, then we'll be back to get you."

"What am I supposed to do?" Tony asked.

"Watch the body," Whitey said. "Just watch the body. You're not supposed to do anything. Take this." Whitey handed him a flashlight.

Tony watched the car disappear down the highway. When it was gone, he turned and went back to the arroyo. He looked at the car, upside down, nose into the ground. The tires looked almost new.

It was getting darker, hard to see. He sat on the bank of the arroyo and smoked the last cigarette in his pack. He should have thought to ask Whitey to bring him a pack from the bar.

He waited a long time. Twice he thought he heard a car coming down the road, but it never came. It was dark now, and he edged closer to the upside down car. It was dark and he felt the need to be near something. He should be home now. He should be on his way to Eleanor, not sitting in the middle of the desert, next to a dead man.

He didn't know how long he waited. It was a long time. It got colder. He wanted a cigarette, he wanted a drink. But mostly he wanted Whitey and Sam to come and get him. Or the Highway Patrol.

"Those guys," he said to the dark. "Those guys just aren't worth much. You ever have friends like that?" He shined the flashlight through the window of the car. The driver hung upside down still, his eyes closed. He looked peaceful enough, not like he had gone through what he had. Except his hair hung straight down, his tie covered part of his face, and his pack of cigarettes just hung in the corner of his shirt pocket.

Tony walked back to the road and looked down it. Nothing. "Jesus," he said. "Jesus, you guys. Come on." It was cold now, and something had gone wrong. They had driven off the highway, or the bar was closed. Something wasn't right. Tony understood he was still a little drunk and he wanted a cigarette. But something just wasn't right. They were supposed to be back a long time ago.

He walked back to the car and sat next to it. He flipped the flashlight on and off a couple of times, illuminating the front fender of the car. He didn't look at the driver. "We're in a hell of a mess, aren't we?" he said to the driver in the dark. In the distance, he heard a car.

He ran out to the road. There, a long way away he saw headlights. He waited. The car disappeared down a dip in the road, then reappeared later, closer to him. When it was close, he waved his arms, thinking it was the guys or the Highway Patrol. The car roared on past him.

Suddenly, he thought he was going to cry. He was alone in the middle of the desert. He thought of Eleanor, waiting for him in Tucson. He should be with her by now. He thought about kissing her. He thought about her skin, warm under the tips of his fingers. Instead, he was stranded in the middle of the desert, alone, with a dead man. He wanted to cry. He wanted a cigarette real bad.

He got down on his knees next to the car, like Whitey had done and he crawled a little forward. He couldn't use the flashlight, because he needed his other hand to brace himself with. He reached in through the window.

He jerked his arm back immediately, like he had touched something sharp or hot. It was only the man's shirt, he told himself. His cold, cotton shirt. He reached back in, felt the man's shirt, and beneath it, his chest, solid and still. He inched his fingers across the shirt until he touched the pack of cigarettes.

Carefully, with just his fingertips, he pulled the pack out. It was nearly full. It was an ordinary pack of cigarettes, not his brand, but a regular pack of cigarettes. There was nothing wrong with it. He shook a cigarette out and put it in his mouth, then spat it out again, as though he could feel the lips of the dead man on his. Then he shook another cigarette from the pack. He lit three matches before he got the cigarette lit. His hand was shaking that hard.

He kept waiting for them to come for him. He smoked three more of the cigarettes.

Finally, the road lit up with the rocking lights of the Highway Patrol car. Behind it came another car. The Highway Patrolman stayed in his car for what seemed like too long, then got out and walked up to Tony. "Well," he said. "Let's have a look."

Whitey and Sam got out of the other car and walked over to Tony.

They stood in a group as the Highway Patrolman crawled down the back of the arroyo and into the window of the car.

"He's dead all right," the patrolman said. "Whew, smells like a distillery in there."

"You need us for anything more?" Whitey asked.

"No. I guess not. Go on home. And, thanks."

"Where were you?" Tony said when they were all back in the car and heading home.

"At the bar," Sam said. "We had to wait for the cop. He was all the way the hell on the other side of the county. We waited for him. We had a couple of beers and waited. Sorry you were stuck out here, kid. Don't let it bother you."

Tony didn't say anything. He just crawled into the back seat and stayed quiet until Whitey said, "Don't take it so hard. We're sorry. Let me have one of your smokes there, kid."

I'll Never Get Out of this World Alive

"I mean Negative capability—this is when man is capable of being in uncertainties, Mysteries, doubts, without any irritable reaching after facts and reason."
—John Keats, 12/21-27/1817 in a letter to his brother

Jeffrey, I say, it is beginning again. You have got that steel guitar in your heart and you are fed up. This is trouble, Jeffrey. You are headed for the depths and you do not swim well. Take hold, boy. Take hold.

Jeffrey is fed up, being in uncertainties, Mysteries, doubts, etc. He cannot read his book, and he cannot write on his paper. Jeffrey boy, you are a good teacher, and a good teacher reads his book and writes on his paper. A good teacher would grab Mr. Keats and Mr. Shelley by the shirt collars and drag them into the classroom where the biscuit brained students would nod and fall asleep as the wimpy old poets caterwaul in counterpoint.

What a good teacher does not do, is sit in some bar—no, not some bar—the very Rodeo Bar where you are now, drinking that whisky listening to that jukebox and rolling dice with the barmaid to see who pays for the music. You are only pretending to write your lecture, and you are fooling no one. No matter how much you like watching those little plastic horses pull that little plastic wagon in the Budweiser sign, that is their work, which they are doing, not yours, which you are not. Get to it, boy. Now.

But I cannot do it. The heft of the Norton in its maroon cloth cover does not thrill me. And I cannot remember what it is you say to students about John Keats. They like the bright, arterial blood, the coughing and the dying. They like to hear about John, caught by a passing Fanny, and seem to regret that he died before he could marry her. But they have no fears that they will cease to be, and they figure anyone who has lived to twenty-five has lived longer than necessary anyway. I do not know how to convince them that a thing of beauty is a joy forever, and I cannot read the lines

> Catch the white-handed nymphs in shady places
> To woo sweet kisses from averted faces—
> Play with their fingers, touch their shoulders white
> Into a pretty shrinking with a bite
> As hard as lips can make it. . .

without looking at the thighs of Sandy Holguin. And I cannot look at the thighs of Sandy Holguin without thinking of John Keats, who wondered

> Were there ever any
> Writhed not at passed joy?
> The feel of not to feel it,
> When there is none to heal it. . . ?

Heel, Jeffrey. Get yourself back to that school, your desk, your book, your paper and that gnawed-on Eberhardt-Faber number three pencil, and work your work. That you are a twenty-nine-year-old English teacher who has discovered that he cannot beat the boredom of his life with a new pair of Tony Lama boots, a G. M. C. pick-up truck, and a Smith and Wesson .357 magnum revolver, and more blues that he has any legitimate right to, means nothing to these darling little children who are expecting you—no, demanding you— to get your tired butt into that classroom and teach them so they may become good, tax cheating, adulterous suburban citizens, and, most likely, make more money than you ever will. It is your duty, son. Write on your damned paper.

I can put part of it together:

> John Keats (b.1795, d. 1821) was the son of a stableman. His were, by accounts, decent people, and though poor, able to send John to school. His father died in an accident when John was eight, and his mother died of tuberculosis when he was fourteen. After his mother's death, John became an avid reader and began to take an interest in poetry. However, only a year later, he was taken out of school and apprenticed to an apothecary, ending his education, but beginning his career as a poet. He published his first book of poems at the age of twenty-two.

What is that you're writing, Carol, the barmaid, wants to know. Carol is a fine looking woman, and I have done a great deal of looking. She could be, if necessary, the Levi Strauss company's main reason for existing. It may be my imagination, but in the last few weeks, she seems to have become more liberal with both her smiles and her pouring.

She has, she tells me, gone to college herself, right here at the community college where I teach, and has even taken Survey of British Literature II. She hated it. What college needs, she tells me, is someone who can translate poetry into English. I find that remark oddly charming.

> By 1816, Keats had committed himself to becoming a poet. In that year he set forth his plan in the poem "Sleep and Poetry": "for ten years, that I may overwhelm / Myself in poesy; so I may do the deed / That my soul has to itself decreed."

The worst thing about working the day shift, Carol

tells me, is that at 5:00 you go home to reruns of *Seinfeld* or the 5:30 news with Tom Brokaw. *Seinfeld* has been stale for years, and Tom Brokaw is kind of cute, but in an uncle-ish way. The thing is, it's no fun to curl up on the sofa with Tom Brokaw.

Wait a minute, Jeffrey. There is more at stake here, I would say, than a lesson plan, which, you will remember, has to be delivered at 9:00 Mountain Standard Time tomorrow morning. There is the further matter of your wife, all questions of her faithfulness put aside for the moment, who is, in fact, a good woman. And, apart from any minor failings she may have in the fidelity department, does love you, need you, and want you home with her. Soon. What is beginning here, Jeffrey, will not make matters any better.

What I like most about a pickup truck is the sense of enclosure. You can haul that several thousand pounds of metal around at a horrifying rate of speed, as I am doing now, the wind catching the tailgate and just demolishing the m.p.g.'s, and the cab just snuggles around you, fitting in close. It is a vehicle that allows you to drive as alone as you are able. There is no empty seat following you, reminding you that there may be others who may want to ride wherever it is you're going. Those with you are next to you. It is an intimate machine.

What is it, Carol wants to know, that you find so interesting in a man like John Keats? Negative capability is what I find. Who could not love a man who wrote something like this:

> Just so may love, though 'tis understood
> The mere commingling of passionate breath
> Produce more than our searching witnesseth:
> What I know not: but who, of men, can tell
> That flowers would bloom, or that green fruit
> would swell

To melting pulp, that fish would have bright mail,
The earth its dower of river, wood, and vale,
The meadow runnels, the runnels pebble-stones
The seed its harvest, or the lute its tones,
Tones ravishment, or ravishment its sweet
If human souls did never kiss and greet?

He said that? Carol asks. Yes. He said that, and there is no need to translate that into English. No, she agrees, what you translate that into is not English. Turn here, she says. It's a small farm road, straight open and dirt. Here, she says, this is my poetry. She takes a cassette from the dash and runs it home. We are doing sixty miles an hour down the farm road that twists and swirls behind us in a sheet of dust. Hank Williams begins to sing through that long and exquisitely fine nose of his:

Your cheatin' heart, will make you weep
You'll cry and cry, and try to sleep.
But sleep won't come, the whole night through.
Your cheatin' heart will tell on you.

And there is poetry there. The steel guitar in that song cries, the way the hardest crying is done—low and steady, faithful behind the other instruments. It keeps at you until you ache with the throb of it all.

I think I could sit through a poetry lecture if it was a lecture on Hank Williams, Carol says. Or Patsy Cline, or Lefty Frizzell. I think about that for a second. Why don't they give lectures like that at the college, she asks.

Hiram Hank Williams was born in 1923, the son of an Alabama lumber camp worker who spent most of Hank's early years in the V. A. hospital. The boy did not like school, and he dropped out at his first chance. Except for the occasional odd job when money was especially scarce, he never worked at anything except playing country music, or "hillbilly" music as it was called then. He remained, for his whole life, an ignorant, semi-literate redneck. That did not obscure the fact that he was a genius who wrote significant, lasting music, though he rarely went beyond the most basic tonic—dominant—subdominant progression in any of his songs.

Here, Carol says. Pull over here. We are about four miles from the highway on the farm road. Both sides of the road are piled high with dirt freshly cut from the irrigation ditches. Beyond the ditches lie long fields of alfalfa in first growth. Carol jumps from the truck, carrying the bottle of Jack Daniels she has taken from the bar. Here, she says, right here, patting the loose soil of the ditch-bank where she has sat.

In the irrigation ditch, water rushes by, pushed by a big green Peerless pump, working about 300 gallons per minute. In the sky above the field, hawks turn as if the air were a bearing machined just for them. Beyond them, the late afternoon sun sends shadows deep into the rock faces and gullies of the Penelenos. I watch the small raptors drift and wheel against the mountains, then descend in excruciatingly beautiful dives to the fields below. Next to me, Carol watches and says only, damn.

Damn, she says again. I guess that's about the most articulate thing you can say about such sights, but I notice that there is a little catch in her voice. Damn, she says once more. He sure got it right, Hank did. From the open door of the truck, Hank keeps singing.

Why don't you say the things you used to say,
What makes you treat me like a piece of clay?
My hair's still curly and my eyes are still blue,
Why don't you love me like you used to do?

She takes a long pull from the bottle and hands it

over. She is crying, very quietly. I'm sorry, she says. I take a good pull and hand it back. Her shoulders are shaking just a little. It's my old man, she says. He left me last month. Just picked up and left. I didn't even think he was slipping around on me.

I take the bottle from her and try to scoot over. But the ditch bank has molded to my butt and I can't scoot. I lean to her. The thing is, she says, he's the third one that's done that to me. Why don't you check and see if there's a sign that says "leave me" on my back? I put the bottle between my knees and pull her toward me. We look like two legs of an easel.

> The news is out, all over town
> That you've been seen a runnin' 'round
> I know that I should leave, but then
> I just can't go—YOU WIN AGAIN

This is a world of fools, I tell her, people who don't appreciate what they have. Some people can't see what's right in front of them.

> Much of Hank Williams' best music, the songs that we remember most—"Your Cheatin' Heart," "Cold, Cold Heart," "I'm So Lonesome I Could Cry," "Why Don't You Love Me," "You Win Again," "I Can't Help It (If I'm Still in Love with You)"—were direct outgrowths of his stormy marriage to Audrey Mae Sheppard, one of his back-up singers, a woman with little talent but an enormous appetite for fame and money.

Hank understood, Carol says. He truly did. My wife is cheating on me, I say. And then I begin to cry, too. She holds me a little tighter. I'm not sure with who, I say. It might be my best friend. We hold each other and rock on the ditch bank.

Hold it just a minute, here, Jeffrey. This whole damned thing is getting way out of hand now. You are leaning too hard on the clichés here, and you are pushing to turn your life into a country western song. You have, you will remember, no proof of that accusation. You have no smoking cigar, no prolonged absences that cannot be accounted for with just a little grace on your part. What you have is a woman of extravagant parts, and I myself would surely miss the sight of her. The smooth slope of her forearm, the grace of hair and eye, the shrug of her shoulders as she shucks her brassiere, the spread of her fingers as she pulls the elastic from her hips are sights that still knock the breath from us, and at last notice, still brought a lump to your pocket.

The only thing you have, Jeffrey, is your damned logical proof. You are capable of cheating on her; therefore, she is capable of cheating on you. That is a cruel enthymeme, boy, one you don't need to support tonight.

Carol puts her head on my shoulder. The smell of her cream rinse is exotic and wonderful. When I was little, she says, we used to walk these ditches for miles. It was the only cool thing you could do, walking in the cold water with the hot sun beating down on you. It was wonderful. It was a wonderful time.

Let's, I say.

Footing is difficult. Where the water has left deposits of silt, our toes find purchase. But most of the way, the bottom is packed clay and slippery. Neither of us are too steady because of the whisky. But we are probably a hundred yards away from the truck and our boots, so far away I can't hear Hank anymore, when she loses her balance and falls backwards. I almost catch her, but I am also trying to keep the bottle from going in the water. I try to pull her up, but I lose my balance, too, and go butt first into the ditch, still holding the bottle up. She is already on her feet when I get to mine. When I try to kiss her, she is spitting ditch water. She walks on. I follow, in love with those wet Levi's.

A thing of beauty is a joy forever
Its loveliness increases; it will never
Pass into nothingness; but still will keep
A bower quiet for us . . .

I hate walking in wet Levi's, she says. They are awful, I agree. They bind and chafe something terrible. We look hard at each other, then lunge. We are in a tangle, trying to get each other's pants down in the middle of an irrigation ditch, in the middle of someone's field, in light that has not fully failed. We thrash in the water. Her Levi's are tangled around one ankle. As I am trying to shimmy them over her foot, she gives a tug at mine, and I go over, backwards and under. When I get up and clear the hair and water from my eyes, she is standing, waiting. I am stunned by the sight of her.

Afterward, we are both covered with mud and dirt, slippery and gritty at the same time. It is more than a hundred yards to the pump and clean water. We gather what clothes we can find. My shirt and shorts are probably at the bottom of the ditch far down stream by now. I try walking the field. These fields are full of rattlesnakes at night, she tells me. I jump back into the ditch. Do they swim, I ask.

I don't know. I guess I never saw one.

The water comes out of the pump cold enough to make our bodies ache. And when we have the mud and sand washed off, there is nothing to dry ourselves with. We go back to the truck and run the heater up as high as it will go. And we listen to Hank Williams.

I got a feelin' called the blues, Lawd,
My heart aches, and a drowsy numbness pains
    My sense, as though of hemlock I had drunk
Since my baby said goodbye
Or emptied some dull opiate to the drains
    One minute past and Lethe-wards
        had sunk . . .

When I wake up, Carol is still asleep. It is completely dark, the moon is out, and I am still drunk. I wake her and we dress. Then I turn the truck and head back. On the road, the headlights pick up a small, dark shape—a house cat, maybe, or a skunk. Carol reverses the tape that has run out.

> She told me not to mess around,
> But I done let that deal go down,
> So pack it on over, tote it on over,
> Move over, nice dog, 'cause a bad
> dog's movin' in.

I reach over and turn it off.

You might as well come in, Carol says when we get to her mobile home. No, I say. It's time to go home. You're in no shape to go anywhere, she says. Stay here. No, I insist. There are things that have to be said, things that have to be settled. I'm sorry. I have to go. She gives me a quick kiss, but says nothing when she closes the door. Back in the truck there is only Hank and me.

> It's hard to know another's lips will kiss you,
> And hold you just the way I used to do.
> Oh, heaven only knows how much I miss you.
> I CAN'T HELP IT IF I'M STILL
> IN LOVE WITH YOU.

The way home is a good ten miles, and about half way I begin to cry. The more I cry, the angrier I get. I turn the volume on the tape deck until Hank's voice distorts and cracks.

> By the time he was twenty-six, suffering from a lung condition and a bad back, John Keats began a steady abuse of alcohol and drugs. He soon developed a reputation for showing up at concert dates drunk, if he showed up at all. Once, in Canada, he literally had be dragged onto the

stage in front of a thousand screaming fans. He stumbled to the microphone, and when his band, the Drifting Poets, began the intro, he seemed unable to recognize the song. Finally, he sang the first two lines of "Ode to Autumn," repeated them three times and passed out. Just two years later, in 1821, living on bourbon and seconals, John Keats went to sleep in the back of his famous white Cadillac and never woke up.

Understand that Jeffrey does not really like guns. They are ugly little things that serve only one purpose when they serve any at all. Yet there is nothing that fits a man's hand quite the way a gun does. Of all the implements a man has ever held, none has been so perfectly designed as an extension of hand and fingers. You need only pick up a gun once, hold it, and get the feel of the thing to know that nothing is ever going to feel that good in your hand again.

When I pull into the driveway, right behind my wife's Volkswagen, my hand goes immediately to the glove compartment. The barrel of the magnum is cold as I slide it into my jeans.

Now aren't you one hell of a sight, Jeffrey, standing in the middle of your yard, shirtless, wet and muddy, defiant as a little mockingbird, waving that gun around and screaming to wake the dead? Don't use that thing, boy. You are pitiful enough as you are.

Even holding the gun with both hands, I cannot steady the barrel. I don't know where the first shot goes. I pull the trigger and there is only muzzle-flash and the sound of the shot with its reverberation. The second shot snaps a limb off the pecan tree in the front yard. Get out here. The third one disintegrates the right window of my pickup truck. Now. Goddamn it. When I hear the front door open, I spin in a low crouch and sight her there, in her robe, barefoot. My feet tangle and I fall. I'm crying loud and hard, and I don't know what happens to the gun.

Jeffrey, boy. Look at your miserable self, I say. For God's sake, boy, don't crawl to her. Crawling doesn't get you there fast enough.

Acts of Contrition

O my God, I am heartily sorry for having offended Thee. I detest the loss of heaven and the pains of hell, but most of all because I have offended Thee, my God, who art all good and deserving of all my love. I firmly resolve, with the help of thy grace, to confess my sins, do penance, and amend my life.
Amen.

Foster, RI, 1989

We knowed it was going to snow. You could feel it in the air. It was like a woolen blanket in that you didn't walk through it, but only dragged it along with you. It was early December, not long after Thanksgiving, and it was in the year of 1927.

So we knowed it was coming, but we didn't worry about it none. Both Paul and me was as at home in the woods as the deer was, and we knowed the ways of deer, too, and we knowed they would be out, gathering up the last of the green before the snow came in. They would be more concerned with eating than they would be with watching out for trouble, which is what Paul and I was for deer. Trouble. Each year we would go out and get ourselves four or five to make it through the winter. It wasn't like it was now. If you needed to eat, you just went out and got yourself a deer. You didn't ask for permission because no one needed to give you any.

We went out around 9:00 in the morning, a little later than we had wanted to because Paul had to take care of some business down to Hudson's where he worked part time. We went out to the southwest around the intersection of Watson and the Plainview roads. It is all houses there, now, but it wasn't back then. Then it was just woods with a few trails that we knowed pretty good. There was a lot of water back in there, springs and swamps and such, and a lot of cover. It was a good place for deer.

There had been a old farm there once, maybe a hundred years before, maybe more than that. You could still see the old stone foundations of the house and barn and plenty of stone walls. I would imagine that most of it is gone now, lost to all the houses they have put in there. Some of those stone walls has been dug out and rebuilt in front of those big new houses they got all over the place.

We hadn't been out for very long, maybe an hour, maybe less, when we found the fresh scat, still warm in your hands in the morning air. It looked like there was five or six of them around, and you could see the trails they used. Deer is pretty much like people, they will walk the same trails through the woods if they have the chance to. So, we started following them, moving slow and steady. We knew we wasn't right behind them, but we wasn't that far off, either.

Maybe it was the snow, which had started by now, coming down steady, in big, soft flakes, but they didn't follow on the trails like we thought they would. We walked for nearly an hour, moving deep into the woods after them, occasionally spotting where they had taken off in some new direction, and us following them, as close as we could.

We knew we had pretty much caught up to them. You could hear the slight rustling in the woods where they was. As you know, there is nothing more quiet than the woods in a snow. The snow was coming harder now, but we had plenty of time to get us a couple and cart them back out before it made the roads too bad to pass.

We weren't speaking now. We didn't need to. We both knew just exactly what we was doing, and if we needed to tell each other something, we would use hand signals. Nothing fancy, just pointing and such. Paul saw a doe first. We were behind one of the stone walls which had a lot of brush and deadfall on top of it, which made it a good place to hide. It made a bad place to shoot from, though, and the deer were getting edgy, moving further into the woods. We also didn't have good sight because of the snow, so that meant we had to crawl over the stone wall and try to get a little closer so we could draw a good bead on the buck, which we had not seen.

Paul went over the wall first, swinging his leg up high to clear the deadfall without making any noise. I did much the same. I was carrying my old Remington 30.06, which was a good gun, but old. It wasn't especially loose in the trigger, but it wasn't a new gun, either. I ain't making excuses, I'm just saying how it was. An old gun and all that.

It was the loudest sound I had ever heard, and it took me complete by surprise. I guess what it was was that the trigger had caught on some of the deadfall, but when it went off, as surprised as I was, I knew what had happened, and right away I knew that Paul had been shot, though he did not cry out as I recall.

I had hunted most of my life, or that small part of it I had lived back then, and I knew the damage that a 30.06 could do. But when I looked at Paul, it near brought my stomach up through my mouth. The bullet had gone in through the back of his thigh and come out the front. It was a fortunate thing that it went straight and just got the leg and nothing more.

Now you would think that there is enough room in a man's thigh that a bullet might pass through and not hit anything more than the meat of the leg. But right away I knowed that wasn't the case. There was little bits of white stuck in the blood in the front of his pants, and I knew that it was bone I was seeing. And blood was coming out everywhere. It was as much blood as I had ever seen at one time, and it was a difficult thing to believe that it was only from a shot to the leg. But I knowed if he kept on bleeding like that, he wouldn't last a long time, so I set to work right away, wrapping my belt tight around the top of his leg to cut off the blood that was running down there, only to spill out onto the snow and steam there.

And that cut the bleeding down some, but it was still coming out pretty good. Paul was awake, but only barely, and just moaning a little with the pain of it all. I took the guns and stuck them up in a white pine tree that was near to keep them out of the snow, and I hoisted Paul up onto my back. He was a big man, near to six feet and weighing over two hundred pounds. I was considerable smaller, going just about a hundred and seventy-five.

But I hoisted him up. I had to work hard at it, because I didn't want his leg to swing free or to drag the ground. He clung on to me, but he would sometimes go out on me and become dead weight. When we had to go back over that stone wall that was no more than three feet high, I seen how hard this was going to be on both of us. I had to put my foot up on top of that wall and try to judge how the weight was going to throw me once I went up on just one leg there. I don't know how long that took, but it seemed like it was a real long time, and Paul letting out these little low moans, though I know he was trying to keep it from me, how much this was hurting him.

It was snowing hard now, and that made things somewhat the worse. It was hard to see where you was going, and the longer we went on the harder a time I had of it, trying to keep up my head. And the ground was picking up a pretty good layer of snow now, even that deep in the woods. I would be a liar if I told you I never stumbled, because I did a couple of times, and once I fell to my knees, but I never let Paul drop to the ground.

When we made it back to where the truck was parked, I got him into the cab and onto the seat, though that hurt him considerable, but at least I knowed he was still alive, though there was still a fair amount of blood coming out of him. And it was a long drive over to Connecticut, because that was the closest place there was a doctor, because the road was full of snow, and trucks wasn't much use in the snow back then. More than once on that trip I wished that we had taken a horse drawn cart, because it would have been better into the doctor's.

And when I got him to the doctor's over in Plainfield, the doctor, he wouldn't have nothing to do with us, because of it was a gunshot wound, and he didn't want to answer to no police about how it had happened. And so, Paul he was getting real bad pale now, and we had to get back into the truck and drive all the way back into Rhode Island where I took him right to the state police, because I couldn't stand it if another doctor turned us away.

And they had a surgeon right there in the barracks, and he done what he could and then they took him on into Centerdale where there was a clinic and he could get the treatment he needed. And he was lucky enough that he lived through it all. It was a strange thing though, because when I got home that night, I had to soak off my shirt, because all the blood had dried and stuck it to my back.

He lived another forty years after that, though they had to take the leg above where the bullet had mashed his bone like that. He never seemed to have held it against me any, but I never saw him and it reminded me of the wrong I had done. And I never went hunting or touched a gun the rest of my life, though it had been my great joy.

Culver City, CA 1976

"I am so sorry. You have to believe me."

She will not look at him.

"Please, please. Please. I never meant to hurt you. I would rather die than hurt you."

"Then, die."

"You don't mean that. Please. Just look at me. See how sorry I am."

Houston, TX 1993

"It is a bad neighborhood," he admitted. "But the food is good. It's some of the best food you can get here in Houston. This restaurant has been here for a long, long time. The neighborhood has just sort of fallen down around it. But it's safe here in the restaurant and right outside. There's security. They're armed."

They had started on the first pitcher of Margaritas, and Allison was sitting next to him, nodding in agreement. It was a bad neighborhood. A very bad neighborhood that had gradually been abandoned by the various groups that had lived and worked here. Now there were a few small businesses open in the daytime only and barricaded at night. The rest had gone over to gangs and drugs. "You're even safe driving over. Did you notice how many police cars we passed?" As soon as he said this, he regretted it. It was already growing dark outside.

Her parents smiled weakly as he explained this. They were trying to be brave and casual about this, but he saw how uncomfortable they were. He should have taken them to a better restaurant in a better neighborhood, he knew, despite the cost. He could have borrowed some money, or he could even have let her father pay, as he had wanted to.

They were good people. He could see that. They were trying valiantly to be pleasant and interested in what he was saying. But they were from Nebraska. Their questions, directed to his art and to his future, were not asked to embarrass him, or to accuse him, but help them find some comfort in this situation. They allowed him to place their orders with the fat waiter who smelled faintly of stale sweat and whose white formal shirt was yellowed at collar and cuff.

Allison was being only small help. She was the one taking offence at every remark, unwilling to see the benign, or at least neutral, in the conversation that limped around the dinner table. When he had offered that he might teach after graduation, bringing a look of hope to her mother's stoically smiling face, Allison had been quick to contradict, to say that he was an artist, and that he should not have to teach to make a living, that he should concentrate on his painting. That it was his duty.

"Then," said her father, showing now the first signs of real irritation. "How can you live? How are you going to eat and pay the rent?"

"I will find ways," he said. "We will be all right. There are always ways to make money."

"It's not just the man's responsibility to make money," Allison said. "Do you think I look helpless? Do you think I can't make a living?"

The fat waiter appeared again and placed their food in front of them. *Tamales, tostadas, chalupas and flautas.* Her father continued to look unhappy, picking at the odd mix of food that had appeared in front of him. Food that must have resembled something he would find himself eating only in a nightmare.

"Your father wasn't suggesting that," her mother said. "He is only concerned about your welfare."

"We won't be on welfare," Allison said.

"It's very authentic. There are lots of Mexican restaurants around, but this one is authentic. It's been here for years. When Mexicans go out to eat, they eat here. They brought the President here last year." He was beginning to realize that Allison was getting drunk, not listening to what was being said, but preparing her next attack on these people.

The mention of the president brought a deeper frown to her father's face, and with it a greater set to Allison's jaw. "It doesn't matter what you think of him, he's the President, for fuck sake."

"There is no call for that kind of language. Your mother certainly doesn't want to hear it, and, frankly, neither do I. I said nothing about the President or politics of any sort. We are having a discussion here. Scott made a comment. I didn't even reply."

"What I was wondering, Scott," her father said. "And I don't mean this in any way bad. It's just that I'm trying my best to understand this. How do you know you're doing the right thing? In your art, I mean. Here's what I'm after. In my business, I have a balance sheet. And that balance sheet shows me how I'm doing. If profits are up, what I'm doing is the right thing, and if they're down, what I'm doing is wrong, and I know I have to do something different. Do you see what I'm saying? What does an artist have to tell him how he's doing?"

The question took him by surprise, but he tried to answer it. "People tell you things, that's part of it. You know if they like what you're doing or if they don't. Most of the time. But it's more a matter of faith, of belief in your own vision, I guess."

"That seems like a hard way to go," her father said.

Allison turned her head in a sharp movement and looked off into the distance to her left, a gesture he knew well, a gesture that dismissed the person in front of her to a kind of conversational oblivion.

"I'm sorry," her father said. "I'm just trying to understand."

No one replied, but the fat waiter waddled over, concerned that something was wrong with the food. He arched an eyebrow, appraised the situation and turned away. "*Margaritas*," he called to the waiter. "*Mas Margaritas, por favor.*" He motioned at the nearly empty pitcher in the center of the table. "You'll never find a better *Margarita* that this one," he said. "We come here sometimes, just for the *Margaritas*. He had a vision of Allison, drunk, staggering out of the restaurant to vomit in the parking lot only a few weeks ago, sure that her parents could see it as clearly as he could.

The parents did not have more *Margaritas*, but he did, and Allison, too, who became more sharp in her defense of him that he thought was unnecessary and uncalled for. The parents became more silent and deferential in a still and formal way, and he poured himself another *Margarita*.

He stumbled a little bit as he went to the restroom, but he was just starting to feel drunk and the stumble surprised him. He wasn't sure how much he had had to drink. In the mirror, his reflection seemed pale and shoddy. His hair seemed now simply unkempt and careless. His new shirt looked cheap and gaudy rather than bright and cheerful as he had originally thought. And he could see himself then as the parents saw him, a young man with no particular prospects, only a vague desire to paint, and not even a clear idea of his own art. He would live off of their daughter and their money and make mediocre art that would cause a very minor flutter at a very minor gallery at a show for which the parents would receive a cheaply printed invitation, but would not come.

He would continue to bring their daughter into the worst parts of Houston, gradually using up all of her money and moving deeper and deeper into more dangerous parts of the city, taking her solace from alcohol and a job that would dead end when he refused to leave Houston, because Houston was an art town, and good art towns were hard to find.

And suddenly, he knew he could not go back and face them again, watch them try hard to be interested and hopeful, to try and find something about him that they liked, or trusted or had some confidence in. He stayed close to the wall on the way out and made his way to the front of the restaurant, and out into the night. It was dark now, but still hot and humid. The security guard was not around, probably taking a leak or a smoke break, and he started to walk, past Allison's car, vaguely toward the center of the city, vaguely toward their apartment. He walked briskly, feeling his legs gather some confidence under him.

Ahead and to the sides of him, far away in the deep dark of the abandoned warehouses and broken buildings, he could hear whistles, back and forth through the dark, like he imagined hunters thousands of years ago had whistled to each other.

Culver City, CA 1976

Her eyes remain unfocused, distant. Though she looks at him, she clearly is looking beyond him, to some point where he isn't.

"What can I do to make this up to you? Just say it. Tell me what you'd like. I was wrong, so wrong. I want to do something, anything to make this up to you. I don't think I could live without you. You're the most important thing in the world to me. Just tell me what you need. What can I do?"

Denver, CO 1997

As they drove north on I-25, the landscape took on a comfortable familiarity, and they felt their spirits rise, coming back after so many years. Denver spread out in front of them as though it had been waiting for them and only them all of these years.

They had lived in Denver nearly thirty years before. She had been married, but not to him though they had known each other well and fallen in love without quite understanding that it was what they were doing.

Nelson had gone to college there, at Denver University, a private school, but the academic poor relation to the University of Colorado only a few miles away in Boulder. He had been a graduate student in biology, studying the signaling of certain fruit eating bats that inhabited the mountains around Denver.

Karen remembered him as a thin, tan young man, somewhat exotic, bearded and unkempt, always in shorts and tee shirts, going off for days and weeks at a time to live in the mountains, only to return unexpectedly at inconvenient times, when he would come over to their house and drink their beer, eat their food, share his pot and to talk animatedly about the thoughts he had kept himself entertained with in the mountains when he was supposed to be observing bats. He had a girl friend, but they did not live together and she did not understand exactly what kind of relationship they had, though she sensed it was mostly and intensely sexual. She thought he came to their house because he and Judy had no ability to talk to each other, despite their intimate familiarity.

She was a school teacher back then, teaching junior high school English, just as she was now, though she thought she might retire soon. She had taught in Denver for fifteen years, which seemed like an extremely long time back then when she was in her twenties. Now fifteen years seems like nothing. Is nothing. He's a teacher, too. High school biology, though in a different district from hers.

Nelson had thought of her as a woman, back then, a woman as opposed to Judy, who he thought was only a girl. Karen was older than Judy, attractive, though less striking than Judy who was tall and blond and graceful as a dancer. He knew how Frank lusted after Judy, and though he understood it perfectly, because everyone he knew lusted after Judy, he found it more amusing than annoying. Karen had known exactly who she was, and seemed to know, too, exactly who he was. On the long nights of smoking and drinking, she would bring out her bottle of Dewar's and her cigarettes, put her feet up on the coffee table, and listen to his wild imaginings quizzically, interrupting him only to say, without taking the cigarette from her mouth, "that's complete, fucking, bullshit." It was, of course, complete, fucking, bullshit and it delighted him to hear her say it, though he would argue as though she had denied the very nature of his existence.

He's trying to find their exit off of I-25, but it seems to be gone. It's actually still many miles ahead, but the city has grown so much since they were last here that his perception of distance is badly off. He is starting to get nervous as the traffic intensifies along with his feeling that everything here is wrong. His good mood is melting away fast.

Denver is the city where he used to laugh. He thinks of it mostly that way. Though he was poor and had some terrible times, especially coming to the realization that he would not ever finish his dissertation on the fruit bats because nothing was especially significant about the signaling of these particular fruit bats, he remembers laughing here. Specifically, he remembers one night with Karen and Frank, when he and Frank started laughing, and caught in the good waves of the dope, could not stop laughing. Karen had stalked off to bed, with him and Frank on the floor, holding each other in their fit of laughter. "I hope you two have a nice life together," she said.

"I was thinking," she said. "About Frank, in that Mustang of his. Just driving up and down the freeway, just for the fun of driving. Can you believe that? Driving because it's fun? It was so long ago."

He's beginning to figure out where he is. "The 1966 Mustang," he says. "He took that thing apart and put it together again, what, twice? How did he know to do that?"

"He just did. He could take something apart, understand how it worked and just put it back together again. He just had to understand everything."

He thinks about the letter they got from Frank two years earlier, outlining the state of his disease, the course of treatment and the probable outcome, which he predicted within two months of his actual death. There was no sorrow or request for pity in the letter, only a detailed and careful study of what faced him as though this were a new and intricate machine he had to understand in order to control. It was as if oncology were his latest hobby, and he and Karen were merely acquaintances who might be persuaded to share his new interest for a while.

"We used to take that road right there up into the hills for picnics. Isn't that the road? Didn't we used to go up there? I think it is. I think that's where we had the picnic. We're not as close to town as I thought."

Her eyes are straight ahead now, her jaw clenched. It is difficult territory, this talk of the picnic.

They had gone, the four of them, he and Judy and Karen and Frank, up into the hills that are now studded with condominiums, to a spot miles past where the road ended. In a grove, by a shallow stream they had eaten, drunk wine, talked and smoked dope. It was the end of summer, they were all back in school, all vaguely trying to hang on to a time that seemed to be passing too quickly. He and Karen had progressed beyond the first stolen kisses and groping behind Frank's back. Karen had begun coming to his apartment when she knew Judy would be working. They were in love and dazed by the sudden, hard reality of it. Frank seemed oblivious, Judy merely disoriented.

Drunk and stoned, Judy had announced, "We could go skinny-dipping in that pool." Both he and Karen watched the widening of Frank's eyes, the twitch at the corner of his mouth.

Frank said, "You first," with a laugh.

Judy had looked at Nelson then, challenging him to say something, to do something to put an end to the notion. "You just want to show Frank your skinny ass," he said. "Go ahead, I think he really wants to see it."

Wounded, Judy turned to Karen. "Come on, Karen. Just you and me. Let's swim."

"It's not a good time for me," Karen said. "You kids go ahead. I'll wait here."

Frank looked surprised and bewildered. "Are we going to do this?"

He had looked at Frank and shrugged.

"Hell yes, we are," Judy announced, pulling off her gauze blouse. "Let's get those duds off." She kicked the sole of Frank's boot. "I mean you, chicken-shit."

Frank looked at Karen, who gave him a shrug and half smile. He pulled off his tee shirt, then his boots. "Come on. Aren't you coming?" Frank asked him.

He looked at Judy, who was pulling off her jeans, her panties pulled down on one side so that a wisp of pubic hair showed at the top. She was staring back at him, challenging. He thought her body was, perhaps, perfect. For a second, he felt her fingers on his flesh, smelled her breath as she slept. He felt a sharp twinge of regret that passed. He smiled at her. "I'm wasted. You go on. I'll wait here with Karen."

Then the jeans were gone and the panties, and Judy turned and stalked toward the little pool, just over the crest of the hill and out of sight. Then Frank was following her, his penis nearly erect and bobbing as he jogged after her.

He got up from where he lay, crawled over and sat next to Karen. Neither of them said anything. He took her cigarettes, and they smoked, pretending not to be listening for sounds they could not hear. It was almost dark when Frank and Judy came back. They made small talk about the chill of the water and the coming dark as they dressed. When they all reached the car, Judy took the seat next to Frank, and when he had started the car and their outlines were just visible in the light of the instrument panel, Karen said simply, "Bastard."

"Judy," he says. He remembers most Karen's anger, which surprised him, because it was genuine.

They had already understood where they were headed at that point, had begun the first few awkward steps of the dance which would change their lives, and he was surprised that she would be so jealous of Frank's attention to Judy or of Judy's desperate need to get the attention. He had covered his own sense of complicity with a small, seething resentment of both Judy and Frank. By the time they reached Denver, everyone had understood that everything had changed, and none of them would be friends again, except for him and Karen.

"Bitch," she says. And he understands that because he has suffered and died, Frank can no longer bear the anger they shield themselves with, but that Judy is still viable.

"I wonder sometimes if she stayed in Denver. I can't imagine she did, but who knows?" He takes the exit for Colorado Boulevard, and, though it has changed, knows now where he is. "You want to drive past the University, or do you want to go on up and find a motel?"

"He's not even buried here. His ashes were scattered in Kansas, where he grew up."

He stays at the bottom of the exit ramp, unsure whether to turn right or left, unsure where they are, or why they have come.

Culver City, CA 1976

"Please," he says. "Please, understand. You have to. You have to understand this." Her eyes open, flicker, then close again, shutting him out.

He kicks her again, in the ribs this time, causing her to roll over, curled into the fetal position. "Please. You dumb, fucking cunt. Can't you understand? I'm sorry."

Small-Block Chevy

These are the true and solemn facts:

It was an accident. Mine for sure, but maybe others, too. I have trouble getting it all straight. They were relatives of Linda's, cousins or in-laws or something. Not blood relatives. I was in love with Linda. I'm hazy on some of the details, but not that one. I was in love with Linda. I am, like I said, hazy on some of it.

It was a Memorial Day party, a celebration of spring. I was out on the lake at their cottage. The old family cottage. I have a cottage on the lake, too. But my cottage is at the other end of the lake, not the rich end. And at that time, Linda was sharing it with me. Theirs is about five times the size of mine, and it has all the conveniences–stereo, t.v., hot tub, computer this and that, indoor plumbing. And they only use it during the summer. My cottage has none of those, except indoor plumbing. I live there year-round, and in the winter, the indoor plumbing freezes solid. But I do all right. Like I said, at the time, Linda was living there with me.

I do all right. I fix things. When you live on a lake, especially a big one with not a lot of access to town, there's always stuff that needs fixing, and I can fix most of it—outboard motors, water pumps, plumbing, electricity and lots of carpentry. The weather on the lake plays hell with everything, but especially wood.

When I can get around in the winter, there's plenty for me to do, fixing things for the summer people who want to have their cottages ready for the summer. Of course, summer is the best time. The summer people come up, find that the pump isn't pumping, the outboard won't start or ice has pulled the fascia off their cottages. I live on my end of the lake, but I make my living on the rich end.

And I didn't really want to go to the party. It was Linda's idea. She works in the town ten miles away in an insurance agency. She does most of the work. The salesmen glad-hand the clients, chat them up, collect signatures, and the rest is up to her. She was having a rough go that winter. She had to get into town five days a week, even when the lake and the roads were frozen solid. Sometimes she would park two miles away and walk home. Lots of times, she walked home across the frozen lake.

So, she was pretty anxious for spring, too. It's a good time, and I understand why she wanted to go to the party. She wanted to celebrate, to relax and forget about winter for another year, laugh and drink someone else's liquor and feel like a human being again, as she explained it to me. And they were her relatives in some way I didn't understand.

It's not really that I dislike these people. But I can't say I like them either.

I don't fit in with them. They have all this old money and a huge cottage that they open the week before the party. And, of course, something fails to kick on, or something else falls off, or the septic backs up. And of course, because it's the week before the party, they call me, understanding I'll come. They have this two page list of things that need to be done. Whatever isn't working to their satisfaction, they expect me to fix. But they pay. They pay slow, but they pay.

The party is going full blast when we get there. If you didn't see the cars out in front, though, you'd never know it. It's the dullest damned party I've ever been to. There's no music or laughter. Mostly people lean into each other and talk and drink. My God, do they drink.

This party started real well, which meant that I made it to the bar before I had to face any of the relatives. They're a friendly bunch. Before we had left the bar with our beers, Chad, the older brother, had Linda in a big hug. He slid one arm from around Linda and gave my hand a shake. It was a smooth move. I admit that. Chad is one of those guys who is just too friendly. He makes a good show of how glad he is to see us. He's not, of course. No one is real glad to see the guy who fixes the toilet. And no one is real glad to see the guy who fixes the toilet walk in with some member of the family, however remote.

But after the hug, Chad gave Linda a big kiss and grabbed me by the shoulder. "Bob," he said. "I've got something to show you. You're going to like this. You're going to like this a lot."

I worked my way out of his grasp. I slugged down the rest of my beer and held up the empty. "I believe I need another beer." Linda shot me a look and shook her head.

"Then let's get some beers," Chad said. "You're going to like this a lot."

And I pretty much did. "It" was a boat, though "boat" doesn't cover it very well. It was more boat than I've ever seen. It was twenty-five foot long and sat low in the water. There was more paint on it than on my house. It had a t.v., radios, a chemical toilet and a deck that was hand-rubbed. I know wood and this was some gorgeous wood.

"What do you think?" Chad asked.

"Looks fast."

Chad took me by the elbow and led me to the rear hatch. Under it was the cleanest, most highly chromed engine I'd ever seen.

"Chevrolet. 350 cubic inch. It cost six thousand dollars. Just for the engine."

Now engines I know. I just put a rebuilt engine in my truck, which has a few more years before the rust gets it completely. A 350 cubic inch. Small block Chevies are wonderful engines, strong and dependable. The one I had put in the truck cost just under a grand. I tried to figure what they had done to make this one cost six.

"Wonderful boat," I said.

"A little later I'll take you for a ride," Chad said. "You and Linda. We'll take a little cruise. I'll show you what she will do."

An hour later I was into my fourth or fifth beer and looking forward to the sixth and seventh. I was also trying to avoid Linda, who had been at me about my drinking, especially around other people.

"The asshole show you his boat?" This was Donny, the youngest son. I wasn't crazy about any of them, but I could tolerate Donny better than the rest. He hung around at Masons', where I liked to have a beer now and again. He was a couple of years younger than I was, and he was a nice enough sort. Never any trouble from Donny. And he'd been known to take a job now and then. Like the rest of us. He's squandered a lot of the money his folks had left him, but he's squandered his on businesses. They were always half-assed businesses—swimming pools, pro-shops, video stores—but they were businesses. He'd tried to make something of himself. All the businesses had gone belly-up, but at least he hadn't spent all his money on big boats, cars and traveling back and forth across country trying to maintain his tan. And I even worked for him for a couple of months, digging swimming pools.

"What's up, Donny?"

He held up his beer can and turned it over. Empty. "Enjoying the party?"

"Sure," I said. "Why not?"

"Costs a fucking fortune. We don't know half of these people. Let's get another beer. Better that we drink it than the rest of these assholes."

It seemed like a good enough idea to me, and we went to get another.

"You see my dog?" Donny asked.

I had seen the dog. It was little more than a pup. It was friendly and handsome. I guess it was a pure-bred German Shepherd, though I really don't know dogs that well. It had been around the party all afternoon, frisking and being everybody's best friend. It was a good dog, and I told Donny that.

"Damned dog is better than anyone else I know. Loyal as hell. Feed him, pat his head, give him a place to sleep, he loves the hell out of you. He doesn't give a damn about anything else. Dogs love you better than your own blood."

I didn't want to hear the rest of this. I could see where it was going, any fool could. I excused myself and went looking for Linda. Even those looks from Linda were better than family stories. I think lots of people in the world hate their families. Decent people keep it to themselves.

Linda was in the kitchen talking to a bunch of people I didn't know. That is I didn't know anyone but Chad. Chad was standing right next to her, and he had his hand on the small of her back. I could tell it was itching to head south.

Now that didn't worry me a lot. Linda and I have had our troubles. Hell, we had been together nearly a year all ready. And we'd worked things out, and we'd pretty much sworn to be faithful to each other. So it didn't bother me that much, but I wasn't all that anxious to let Chad grab a free feel, either. I moved up on the other side of Linda.

"Now, here's a man who knows his boats," Chad said when he saw me. "Bob, tell Linda about the boat. Tell her what kind of boat I just bought."

"Real nice boat," I told Linda.

"Real nice?" Chad said. "Real nice? You know how much that boat cost? More than my Mercedes, that's how much it cost. And the Mercedes cost eighty thousand. You've seen my Mercedes haven't you?" I had, but he wasn't talking to me. He was looking straight at Linda and leaning into her. I leaned back to check the progress of his hand.

"It's a great car," Linda said. "It's a fucking great car."

Well that stopped me. I mean Linda is a grown up woman and she says "fucking" as often as anyone else. She says it a lot when she's disgusted, when she talks about her job—her fucking boss, the fucking clients, the fucking paperwork—that sort of thing. But this wasn't that sort of thing. There was something in the way she said it that made me think she wasn't disgusted at all.

Chad leaned harder into her. "It's a fucking great boat," he said, just above a whisper.

Well, that did it. I had to get out of there. We had an agreement, Linda and I, and I had to trust her on this, and remember my part of the agreement—that I wouldn't cause any trouble. At this point, I figured Linda was better able to keep up her end of it than I was.

Outside, there was the usual assortment hanging around in chinos and Topsiders, their sweaters knotted around their necks. I never understood that. Either wear your damned sweater or take it off. So, what are you into? One of them asked me. Beg your pardon? What do you do for a living? What are you into? Lumber and hardware, I said because that was pretty much it. I headed for the bar again.

Donny was under the bar. I mean it. He was on his hands and knees, under the bar. I gave him a nudge with my foot, figuring he was a lot drunker than I was. You seen my dog? he asked.

"Good dog."

"No. I mean, have you seen my dog? Around here? I haven't seen him for a while."

I hadn't, but I volunteered to help him look, glad for the excuse to be doing anything that didn't involve standing around trying to talk to people I didn't want to talk to.

And I was looking for the dog when I rounded the corner of the cottage and came on Judy. Judy was the sister, the middle one. A few years ago, Judy was about ten miles past pretty. Now she's just that. Past pretty.

Judy was sitting on the ground, her knees up and her arms crossed over them. Her dress had slipped to about mid-thigh. She took a sip of her gin and tonic and looked at me. "What the hell are you doing out here, Bob?"

I knew what she was asking, but I just said, "Looking for Donny's dog."

"Jesus Christ. That damned dog. You'd think it was something important, not just a mutt he'd picked up at the pound."

That made me feel better. There was something about this family I could get a hold on. One of them took mutts from the pound.

"Donny and his fucking dog. Chad and his fucking boat. What a couple of assholes." She took another drink and looked at me. I tried not to look at her legs. Then I tried not to think about her panties. "Pull up a seat," she said, indicating the ground next to her. "Take a load off."

"Well, Donny's dog is lost."

"We wish. Sit. The damned dog will come back. He always does."

I should explain here that I have a history with Judy. It's a short history, but a lot of people know about it. And my history with Judy is only one of a lot of histories Judy has. But I'm a little careful around her.

I sat down next to her, but not too close. "He's run off."

"Smart dog," she said. "He wants out of the family like the rest of us, but he keeps running back. I can't for the life of it figure out why. Bunch of assholes, this family. You think we're assholes, Bob?"

"Nah" I said. "I don't think so." I wanted to tell her I was at the party with one of the family.

"Bunch of assholes. Goddamned bouquet of ass-holes. Every goddamned one of us."

"Now, Judy, you shouldn't be saying things like that." And I reached over and put my arm around her shoulder.

Now I admit I shouldn't have done that. It was a bad move, but I meant it. I mean the right way. I didn't mean anything but sympathy by it.

But the next thing I knew, I had an armful of Judy, then a lapful. Then a mouthful.

I don't mean to excuse myself in any of this, but I didn't intend it and I pulled away as fast as I could. But it's a strange thing here. I mean there she was, lying across my lap, looking at me like I had just kissed her, which I had. But she was also looking at me like I was going to kiss her again, which I wasn't.

It was an awful moment. I mean I had pledged to be faithful to Linda, and I figured she was probably being faithful to me. But Judy was in my lap with her dress all up. And she wasn't that far past pretty. And I didn't have to wonder about the panties anymore. But Linda was inside with Chad, and we had just pledged to be faithful to each other. We were both drunk at the time, but we had meant it.

Well, I didn't kiss her again. Well, once more. But then I wriggled myself free and started to get up.

"Where are you going?" she asked me.

"Donny's lost his dog. I've got to help him. Besides I came with Linda. I guess I ought to find her, too."

"Linda?" she said. "You came here with Linda? Christ." She rolled over onto her belly and looked up at me. She still hadn't fixed her dress. It was quite a sight. "Forget about the dog. And you can forget about Linda. You know what they say — 'If you love something, let it go. If it loves you, it will come back.'"

"What about Linda?"

"Forget it."

"No. What about Linda?"

"Chad's hot for her that's all. He has been for years.

Don't worry about it, he's an asshole. Stay here. We'll talk. Fuck them. That's what families are for, to fuck each other."

"No," I said. I headed back into the house.

Chad had Linda in a corner of the kitchen, leaning into her. He wasn't doing anything you could see, just crowding her. Linda saw me and rolled her eyes. I raised my eyebrows. You know, to ask her if she wanted me to step in. She shook her head, no, with that look of disgust she's given me a few times. The one that says I don't approve of this, but I'll deal with it.

So, I knew everything was O.K. I pushed past them to get a drink of water at the sink. Suddenly I wanted to be a lot more sober than I was. Funny how you work so hard to get drunk and then you work a lot harder to get sober, only it doesn't work as well. That's when I noticed her hand was on his hip, maybe in his belt. I thought about what that meant, was she pulling him toward her, or pushing him away? Pushing him, I thought. Then I thought that remark about families fucking each other, and I got confused. Push or pull? I stepped in, put my arm around her, smiled at Chad and pulled her out the door.

"Jesus, Bob," she said when we got outside.

"Jesus has nothing to do with this. We're getting out of here."

"Bob," she said. "I hate it when you get this way."

"Me? Chad was on you like white on snow."

"Chad's drunk and you are too, I think. There's nothing going on except that you're about to make a scene. You're not going to make a scene are you?"

That one got me. I've made a few in my time. And I've regretted it afterwards. And Linda's regretted a few of them with me. Maybe I was pretty drunk, but I knew I didn't want to make another scene. "Let's just go home," I said.

"No," she said. "I'm going back into the kitchen and talk to people. You're going to behave yourself. I love you." Then she reached up and kissed me. It was a lot different than Judy's kiss, and it set me right.

I was on the patio, away from everyone else, drinking diet Coke and behaving myself. I wasn't talking to anyone, and I was feeling pretty good. I was coming around and knew that I had been pretty drunk, but I was O.K. now. "Bob," Donny said. "You've got to help me."

"The dog will come back," I said, remembering what Judy had told me.

"Not this time," Donny said. "He's down on the point, and he's stuck out there. He can't get back."

"He got out there, Donny. He'll get back. Dogs are pretty smart."

"He's not a dog, Bob. He's a pup. It's a long swim from the point over to here, and look at the chop on the lake. You want my dog to drown, Bob?"

The point is about a half a mile from the cottage. It's all rock and juts out into the lake about fifty yards. The back end of it is all gully and briar. I've been out there a couple of times in a boat and I couldn't make my way to the road from there. "How the hell did he get out on the point?" I asked.

"I don't know. But he's there and he can't get off. We got to go get him."

We walked out to the beach. It was pretty dark by then, and I couldn't see the dog, but I could hear him. He was howling away like a lost soul. It damned near broke my heart. He was stuck all right.

"If he got out there, he can get back," I said. "Besides we'd need a boat to get out there."

"We'll take Chad's boat."

I looked out at the boat, moored at the dock. It was a beauty. The idea had some appeal, I admit. I thought about the small-block Chevy, all brand new and hopped up to the tune of six thousand dollars. I thought about all the ponies it could put out. "It's your brother's boat," I said.

"Right. Let's go."

What the hell. It was his brother's boat, not a stranger's. I'd be just along for the ride. And Chad had promised me a ride.

"Let's go," I said.

"You'll have to run it," Donny said when we got to the boat. "I'm fucking smashed."

"I've had as much as you. I think you better run it."

"You're pretty sober," Donny said. "I'm smashed on my ass. It will be safer if you run it. You're good at this sort of thing."

Well, there it was again. Whenever things were not quite perfect, hire good old Bob to fix them. I wasn't going for it. "I don't know this part of the lake. You do. You run it."

"No," Donny said, "I think Chad would like it better if you ran it. He's not real crazy about me messing with his boat."

Well, I wasn't real crazy about the idea. If Chad didn't want Donny running his boat, he probably didn't want me running it, either. Still, I wasn't part of the family, and he probably didn't hate me as much as he did them. I thought of him in the kitchen with Linda and her hand on his belt. Pushing or pulling? And then I listened to the pup, howling way out on the point. I didn't like this, and I told Donny that.

"Look," Donny said. "I'm plastered. Shitfaced. Snockered. I'm bad drunk, man. There aren't any rocks until close to the point. Slow down as we get near the point. I'll hop out and get the dog. We'll be fine."

And we were. I was sober enough to be real careful. Even when that small-block Chevy roared to life, I kept a soft hand on the throttle easing it out into deep water, and even in deep water, I kept it down.

It worked just like it should. Donny hopped out of the boat, real graceful for a drunk, scooped up the pup and we headed back.

"See what it will do," Donny said. "We have good clear water all the way back. Open it up. Go on."

I thought about it. It was tempting, but it wasn't my boat, wasn't my part of the lake. I thought hard. Push? Pull? And I pushed, pushed the throttle to full open. I hadn't even begun to wind her out when I heard it scrape and went head first into the windshield. I didn't know the rock was there. I couldn't know it. It wasn't my part of the lake.

I was O.K. We all were. I wasn't really aware of anything until I was swimming for the bank and saw that Donny was just ahead of me. We stopped and treaded water, and I looked back where he was pointing.

The bow was just going down, and in a second, there were only ripples where the boat had been.

"Jesus Christ," Donny said. "You just tore the hell out of my brother's boat. You sank his hundred-and-fifty-thousand-dollar boat."

I was just starting to see how much misery lay ahead of me, when a dark shape brushed by me in the water. And I knew in that moment what Donny had known all along. That goddamned dog could swim like a goose.

Ball Hawks

Early morning, the sun just up. The grass, heavy with dew, looks, from this angle, silver in slanting light. They are already out, notes written on the backs of receipts, of deposit slips and papers headed "From the Kitchen of," left at the starter's shack. They play on year passes bought from the city. A year of unlimited play for two hundred dollars. These are men who have known what it means to be poor. From the shack to the first tee, their traces are the three sets of dark green footprints disappearing across the silvered grass.

There are always three, barring flu, catarrh, arthritis, diarrhea and visits from children. They have hit their drives and second shots. Drives at one forty, one sixty two, one fifty seven, second shots much the same. The shots off an odd collection of clubs, old and new. Ancient Mizunos and Northwesterns, pulled from the bargain barrel in the pro shop. Eight dollars each. Big Berthas and Bubble Burners, a couple of hundred dollars each, from assorted kids—Spokane and Pittsfield, Syracuse and Düsseldorf, sent at Christmas and birthdays. "It's a beaut, for sure, but I'd be a son of a bitch if I would spend that kind of money on a golf club."

The balls then. All three of them, still one hundred yards out. One near the center of the fairway, one fairway left, the last in the right rough, second cut. Get it on in three and roll it in for par. A DDH from Walmart, $15 for the 18 pack, an orange Top-Flite, a

Slazenger fished from the water in front of the third and sixteenth. "Lookit that. Brand spanking new." The logo a leaping cat. "Ain't just the prettiest little pussy ball?" This last to be repeated until the ball is lost again, in the water or the thick rough next to five.

They keep walking, talking in the short distances of the fairway, for they are all in the fairway, speaking loudly to be heard over the silence of the early morning course. They bracket the green. They fire away from the fairways. They surround the green. "Let it happen, Captain." "Fire at will." "That one puts me in the brig for sure." They keep their backs straight and walk from their heels. They have in their day known Corregidor, Anzio and Choson Reservoir. They have shrapnel, night sweats and government disability. They march down the fairways. Old golf shoes, Addidas walkers, crosstrainers, strapped on with Velcro. Their legs white and lumpy and hairless in the morning light. They are wrapped for the arthritis. Knees, ankles and wrists, backs and elbows. Ace elastic bandages and techtonic magnets in rubber wraps. A copper bracelet at the wrist.

The balls they have struck spin clockwise, counter and back to front, landing and running, rarely straight, but skidding left to right and, one, right to left, coming to rest against the tall grass of the rough and behind a white pine that blocks the way to the green. He comes up, wobbling on his ankles (one four-year-old Foot Joy missing two spikes under the ball of the left foot). His head appears from behind the trunk of the tree, disappears, appears again. From across the fairway they sing to him, "Oh, Danny Boy, the trees, the trees they are calling."

He rummages through the bag for the club that is best for this, though he is not sure what "this" is. It is through the tree or past the tree, or before the tree. He is still tangled in dreams, as though they are thin and sticky, and he must peel them from himself. He has dreams of iron and brass and clay, of his own body turning into brittle metal as he sleeps. He is transformed by night and spends his days trying to know what it all means.

He shakes his head, fishes a wadded Kleenex from the pocket of his shorts, blows his nose and looks again. "I've seen worse," he says. Three years ago, he sat in a leather chair and squinted at the dark film. He was not sure what he was supposed to see, never having seen his own body from the inside before. "Right there." A ball-point pen held delicately in the fingers, not quite touching the surface of the film. "Right there at the tip of the pen." A dark spot, the size of a dime, maybe less. "That's where it is. That's what we've got to get out of there."

And there is the cutting, but that is not enough. After the cutting, the chemo, that takes his strength, his hair, his appetite. He drops forty-six pounds. Days he lies in the bed, picking at the chenille coverlet, watching the shapes quiver and move across the television set. In the sickness, the vomiting, the standing and falling, he hears the voices call out to him, "Oh, Daniel, are they able to deliver you?"
Now he disappears into the trees, hole after hole.
"Where is Danny gone?"
"Back to water the trees, again, I suspect."
He comes out of the trees, shaking his head. "One cup of coffee, good for eight pisses, now."
"Check your zipper, there, Sarge, something is liable to fall out."
He adjusts his pants and shrugs. "Dead men don't jump out of fourth-floor windows."
He takes a seven iron from the bag. A small swing, the club never raised past the hip. The ball rises up, six feet, eight, then drops twelve feet away, in the fairway,

bounces, rolls, then comes to rest. Out from behind the trees he hobbles on shaky ankles, his hair coming back long and white. And he thinks maybe he will not cut it, having been delivered now, back and safe, among the rest of them. In his life, happier now, astraddle waking and dreaming.

They carry with them the smells of the medications they have rubbed in before starting off. BenGay and Aspercreme, Capzasin, Aloe Vera, Pazo and Noxzema. They are also filled with Dimetapp and Metamucil, Xanax, Prozac, Cardizem, Sular, Hyzaar, Pravachol, Lovastatin, Procar and Lasix. Coming out of the Nytol, Sominex, and Smirnoff, bolstered with McDonald's coffee and hashbrowns, Dunkin' Donuts' Bavarian Creme.

They play teams, each teaming with Jimmy who shoots always his last score, always the 93 he shot two weeks before Christmas, three, maybe it was four, years ago. Today it is Daniel and Lemuel against Samuel and Jimmy. Always for the coffee at the end of the round. One dollar and seventy five cents grudgingly paid for the pale coffee, greedily drunk.

Between the footprints, the twin lines of the pull carts—Bag Boy and homemade. The bags are old, vinyl, nylon and canvas lashed to the carts with red and yellow bungee cords, gray duct tape and yellow polypropylene cord. From the handles of the carts, bags of week-old bread for feeding the ducks and pigeons, the huge catfish, fat from eating baby ducks, coming up from the bottom like sharks, plastic grocery bags for the balls they will find in the roughs and the ponds. With their retrievers, they fish for the balls hit in since yesterday morning, Titleists, Top-Flites, Pinnacles, some nearly new. They tally up the balls as they tally up the pars and bogeys and double bogeys. "I'd sure like to find me some more of that pussy."

"I believe Jimmy would just like you to find a game in there somewheres, old friend. If I was missing putts as bad as that, I believe I would take that new putter out of my bag and see what it can do."

"It can miss them as bad as this one. It don't make no difference. Titanium, Balata. It's the putter, not the putter."

"What do you suppose that putter put him back?"

"I can't even stand to think. The boy knows how to spend money. I've never seen a soul better at it, not even his mother. Nothing more than a pot to pee in, but a gold plated one."

"Things are no better, then?"

"It never occurred to me that he would just ruin the whole goddamned business. Should have known. Should have, should have. Pup never missed a meal in his life because he had a bitch for a mother and a dumb mutt for a dad. I learned to be a man freezin' my frig off and starvin' near to death in Korea. Swore he'd never know what it meant to be hungry. Guess I got what I wanted."

"Sometimes you got to learn whether to eat the eggs or the hen. That's a hard lesson. He does send you nice presents, though."

"You like this damned putter so much, you can have it."

"No, I got troubles of my own. Keep yours in your own bag, old Sammy."

"At least Jimmy don't ever let me down."

"Never does. Not no more."

The bags are stuffed with balls, scrounged from the course, nearly new, once waterlogged. Top-Flites and Titleists, Maxflis and Hogans, Pinnacles and KroFlites. They are orange and yellow and mostly white. They trade them by their color. "You like them punkin balls. Give me a Titleist, and I'll give you both of them." The rest of the pockets stuffed with Band-aids and aspirin, old gloves, *The Rules of Golf*, 1974 edition, score cards partially filled out. Cans of Coke and Sprite. Lighters and cigarettes and in one bag a five pack of Antonio and Cleopatras. ("I smoke them out here and the old woman she doesn't know, though I don't think she could smell a sack of shit if she stepped in it anymore.") A bottle of nitroglycerin tablets, Pepto-Bismol and Kao-pectate. (You walk in three holes out with a pants full, you'll know what I'm talking about). Power Bars and Snickers, crackers and half an apple, dry as a wood chip.

They move across the green, old putters in their hands, the grips disintegrating. From 20 feet, nine and six, they bend over the putts, heads down, and they are quiet, like women at prayer. From 20, the first spins at the cup then drops. From nine the putt holds the line and never drops but slides by eight inches. The six curves up slightly, leaving a gentle arc on the wet grass, to the cup, like the end of the rainbow.

"If you keep on putting like that, that coffee is going to taste especial good when you buy it."

"I could find another cup says Jimmy will birdie eighteen and neither of you will."

"He always does, and we never do. Must of died a happy man."

"I believe he did. I'm thinking I'm coming up on a birdie there myself."

"Nah. Come on, old sport. Buck up. You got to keep bogeying it, just like the rest of us for a while yet."

And on to the next tee, a quick stop in the woods to lose the last cup of coffee and look for balls. Deep in, through the briars and under the brush, a Pinnacle Gold, slightly discolored on one side. "God must of hit that one in when He was just a tot." Around the tee box, the gleaning of the tees, tossing away the broken with a quick back flip of the wrist, the two good ones gathered in and deep in the pocket. "When I run out of tees, I quit the game."

The numbers rise, hole by hole, the card weighted with them. It will be poured over, nudged and adjusted, each number the beginning of a story. Then it will be tucked away in a glove compartment or in the pocket of a coat or in the drawer of an ancient desk. But the numbers are the numbers. Neither the totals of desire or deceit, but the numbers, given, solemn, among the joking. "It looks like Jimmy is the best player on your team again, Sammy."

"That's because Jimmy doesn't ever have to pay for the coffee. Six," he says, shaking his head as if to erase this number. And a hand on the other's shoulder. "The wife, Lem. How is the wife?"

"Yesterday, pretty good. Today, who knows?" When he has hit the last ball, given his score, drunk the coffee it seems certain he will pay for, offered to buy more, he will get behind the wheel of his seven-year-old Buick and drive to where his wife is, *La Casa en los Sombres*, the House in the Shadows, and woo her again, as he has for several years. He will woo her to eat, to fix her eyes on some point he might find in the small room, where the others pass in and out, to know it is him and, still, her. He holds in his hand that which is more precious, tracing with his finger the lines in her hand he has held for forty six years. He looks at the eyes which roam beyond where he cannot see or go, and he cannot hold them or stop their endless roll and wobble. He blots the saliva from the mouth he has kissed more times than he can remember.

In her hands he can trace his life. What esteem he has, she has made with these hands that move idly now, lost in her lap, anchored in his fingers. And this is his anchor, too. Released from her hands, he drifts into his day, cooking poor meals he can barely eat, wouldn't like if he could, cleaning the house that rings as hollow as brass, but has been paid for for more than ten years, reading what means nothing to him and listening to the quiet babble of the television in the background.

And when her eyes finally catch on his, she swims back from the gates of memory, and she holds him there. She speaks with the kind tongue of the law, smiling at his shining head. "Lemmy, you have grown so old." And he ages as she retreats, only their hands holding them together as time disjoints and separates.

He brings the driver down in a smooth arc, sending the ball spinning into the long grass of the rough on the right. "That one won't kill you," Daniel offers. Lem hoists his regret. "I just can't finish. I don't know why I can't, but I just can't finish. I just can't get that damn thing to go into that little hole there."
"That's because putting isn't golf."
"If putting ain't golf, just what is it?"
"Croquet."

They move through the fairways laterally, going from rough to rough, their tracks fading in the sunlight. Their shots arc up, under hit, fat and thin, club faces open and shut, spinning counter and clockwise, waterlogged and bouncing and running off at odd angles. They end up mostly in the fairway. They bag their clubs and swear. They bogey and double bogey and par. They fish the balls others have lost, tee them up, and hit, watching them wobble and spin in the now unfamiliar air. They limp after them, turning luminous in morning sun.

Adultery

"Don't point."

"I was just showing you, that's all."

"It's not our business, not mine, not yours. It's one of the reasons people come to bars. It's one of the main reasons. Watch the ball game."

They were up, four to one, but the pitcher was starting to fade in the heat. "What's going to happen is that they're going to bring in Norton, and then there goes the whole game. You're going to see runners going around the bases like water going down a drain. Then we're all going home. Enjoy this while we're still able."

"I'm just saying, it's like amateur night over there."

"No. In the northern hemisphere, water goes around clockwise. In the southern, it's counter clockwise. It's going to be like water going down a drain in Australia. In baseball, the runners move counter clockwise. Which is odd, when you think about it."

"What the hell are you talking about?"

"The pitcher. Muñoz. He's fallen behind the last four batters. He's dead. Nobody's told him yet, that's all."

"Look, she's married. That's for dead certain, and I got twenty that says he is, too. We ought to just go over, stick them in a cab and send them on their way. They're driving me nuts."

"Then don't look."

"Don't you think it's odd how in baseball the runners move counter clockwise? I mean this is a clockwise society."

Larry, the oldest of them, shook his head. "Look. It's Saturday afternoon. We had a decent round of golf. Now we're sitting in a nice bar, drinking beer. We're not mowing lawns, cleaning gutters or painting anything."

"Right, like Pete's probably doing right now."

"That's right. Don't fuck it up."

"Who's fucking anything up? I was just saying. They're a couple of first timers. Somebody take pity on them and strap them together. And I got fifty bucks says that one of them gives up and just leaves. In the next half hour."

"I was talking baseball," Art said. "It was Don who got on the couple at the bar. And I'll take that fifty, because it's so easy. It's the easiest thing in the world. They'll figure it out, somehow."

Larry looked over at the couple. They had moved together a few minutes ago. He was balding and going to pudge. She was more or less pretty, though plain. She was forever pulling at her hair. They were talking, but they hadn't really started the lean yet. "You were talking some kind of theory that's baseball only by the wildest stretch of the imagination. Who cares whether they go clockwise or counter clockwise?"

"He's right though. It is amateur hour."

It was February, a cold front had moved down from Canada and settled in. The ground had been frozen for a couple of weeks, and the sky was leaden gray. They had had a couple of snowstorms, but mostly they got short spurts of blowing powder. It felt like that today, though the air was dry and crisp. He pulled his coat closer to him and pulled the collar up to cover his neck. He wished he had chosen a warmer spot. The wind whipped around his gabardine trousers, and the thin soles of his Ferragamos sent the chill straight up his legs to the base of his skull.

It was a small city park, surprisingly crowded in the early afternoon. A bunch of school kids roamed the far end of the park with their teacher, looking at trees and bushes. Their voices rose and fell in the afternoon air. The big yellow school bus they had come on was parked at the far end of the nearly empty lot. The kids and he were alone except for a couple of elderly walkers who huffed across the distance, bundled and red faced, working with everything they had against the cold, and, he guessed, not too distant death. Around the pond there were a couple of Canada geese who had been too lazy to head south. They huddled by the shrubs and did not move as he paced back and forth, trying to ward off the cold. He wished he had picked a warmer spot for this.

He saw her car as it turned into the parking lot. He had known her for a couple of years. She and her husband were friends of friends. They had met at a party, and he had taken a shine to her immediately. He thought of it just that way. "He had taken a shine to her." They had seen each other a few times at parties and once in the grocery store. He thought maybe she liked him, too, but she was quiet and reserved. Elegant in a way, he thought. A little more wry and sophisticated than his wife. And she was small and graceful in her gestures. Years before she had been a dancer. They had been lovers for three months now after he had made an awkward pass at her at their friends' house. She had cocked an eyebrow at him and said, "Shut up. Call me when you're sober." Then she had stalked out of the kitchen. He had thought about that the rest of the night. He called her the next day.

She smiled and waved as she brought her Volvo into the spot next to his Dodge. He had always felt a little funny that her car was nicer than his. She got out of the car wearing jeans and sneakers under her fur trimmed coat. She kept tugging the coat up. She had to get up on her toes to give him a quick kiss. He put his arms around her and pulled her to him. "Jesus," she said. "Maybe there's no time for a room, but a restaurant would have been nice."

"I thought the park. Let's take a walk. We'll warm up."

"Right. Let's move before I freeze my ass off. You would care about that, wouldn't you? If I froze my ass off?"

He pulled her closer to him, making it difficult for both of them to walk. "I care about all of you, I really do. But yes, I am extremely fond of your ass."

"Silver tongued devil."

He took her hand in his, a gesture that was surprisingly intimate, though they were both wearing Thinsulate gloves.

She stopped where the geese were huddled under the shrubbery. "I don't know why they didn't fly south. They're miserable. Look at them."

"Maybe they didn't have enough frequent flier miles."

"I bet right now they're thinking that this was a bad decision. Staying over for the winter. If they could think."

"Flying rats," he said. "They learn to live on garbage, and then they don't leave because the garbage is here and it's plentiful. They ought to let poor people come out and shoot them. Solve a lot of problems at once."

She said nothing, only let go of his hand, then snaked her arm through his and retook his hand, pulling them closer together.

"So you see," the teacher said. "There is a lot going on in the winter. And over here are geese who stay through the winter now." The teacher, in a hooded parka and big mittens, made sweeping, padded gestures as the students walked, ran, skipped and stumbled up to her. Some of the kids looked at them as they passed. A couple of them giggled. Grown ups out in the park in the middle of the day, holding hands. Two boys shoved each other, laughing. "Hey," one of the kids said. "You going to fuck her?" They laughed and ran off toward the others.

He felt himself redden. She tightened her grip on his arm. "Cute kid, huh?"

"Damned kids know too damned much these days."

He felt his pulse quicken, his stomach begin to churn. He hadn't been able to eat for a couple of days. He wanted this over, but he was too nervous to broach the subject. He pulled her to him a little closer, and she leaned her head against his shoulder. He liked the touch of her, the smell of her. With her he felt a slow, easy pleasure that he hadn't known in a long time, even now, her presence was calming, comfortable.

"So," she said. "What's up?"

He saw the opportunity open in front of him like a flower, and then, as though in time-lapse photography, it closed again. He stalled, paralyzed by lack of courage.

"It's so cold."

"This wasn't a good idea. I see that now. Let's go on back to the cars." They turned and made their way back, past the pond and the geese, toward the gate of the park where the children and their teacher waited.

"Do you want to go get a drink? Some coffee?"

"No," he said. "I guess I don't."

She stopped then, right at the entrance gate. "This is it, isn't it? You brought me out here to tell me you're not going to see me anymore, didn't you? Didn't you?"

"I'm not good at this," he said. "I mean the sneaking around. The lying. It's just too hard for me."

"And you suppose I like it any better? You think it's easy for me?"

He took her arm and tried to move her past the gaggle of children at the gate. She wrenched it away and stalked out the gate. The children and the teacher all looked at them like they were something surprising and strange. He followed after her, trying to catch up, trying to formulate some way to say this to make it better. "I'm sorry," he mumbled. "I'm really sorry."

"Sorry," she said. "Sorry. Well, I'm sorry you're

sorry. This must be a terrible inconvenience for you. You got what you wanted, and now you have to clean up the mess. That's what it was, wasn't it? I was a conquest. A piece of ass. You got it, and now you have to dispose of the rest of me. You son of a bitch."

"No," he said. "No," holding the last, nearly keening. And even in his denial, he understood the truth, that no matter how much he liked her, no matter how much he enjoyed the presence of her, he had been looking toward this moment from the first time he had touched her, from the first time he understood that she was going to sleep with him. He had entered into the relationship, looking for a way out, like a man plotting a military campaign or a bridge move.

"Come on," he said. "Get in the car. Let's talk in the car."

"I will not get in the car, and I will not talk to you. You're not going to talk yourself into some false nobility here. You piece of shit."

"Don't. No. Please." He was aware that the school bus had moved up from where it had been parked to stop at the gate to load the children. "Not out here in the open."

"Not in the open? So the whole thing will just be between us? No one else will know? No one will know what a shit you are? No one will know that you're a lousy, lying motherfucker? You don't want anyone to know that? You don't want anyone to think badly of you? You fucker, you fucker."

In his worst imaginings, he had not imagined a scene quite like this. He thought to run, to turn and get into his car and get the hell out of there, but now the school bus had blocked him in, trapped his and her cars in front of it. He shook his head, no. No. And he felt the tears start. And when they did, she hit him.

"Don't you cry, you cocksucker. Don't you dare cry." She hit him again. "Shit licker. Butt fucker. Piece of shit bastard." And with every word, she swung her fists, sideways, awkwardly, but hard, and he bent down to cover himself. And when he did, she began hammering his back with her fists. And then he went down to his hands and knees. And she kicked him once, hard in the ribs.

"Please. Please. Stop it. Stop this. The children. There are children." And he looked up to see that the teacher in her parka and mittens was standing between them now, pushing her back, away from him. And as he got up, he saw the children, their faces pressed up against the glass, looking on in amazement as their teacher held back the screaming, cursing lady, while the man stood up, shaking, his pants torn, his coat dirty, crying.

"Don't let him point to the left hand. Please, God. Not to the left, to the right. Aw damn, it's Norton, they're bringing in Norton. Aw please, somebody. Pray for rain, for God's sake."

"Uh, oh. Uh oh. It's heating up. Check it out."

"He doesn't lose every game. He's six and four."

The man was leaning in closer on her now, and she wasn't moving away. She had stopped pulling her hair and had begun chewing on her lip.

"What did I tell you? What did I tell you?"

"Would you please just ignore them? Watch the game."

"Yeah. Good idea. Watch Norton warm up. Watch Norton for the only time he's not going to have the ball hammered right back at him. Watch Norton while he has a lead."

"I told you they'd figure it out. Are you ready to cough up the fifty?"

"Just keep the ball down. Keep it down and keep it in the park, you worthless bastard."

He was running the dog on a thirty-foot lead, letting him take all of the rope, then calling him back with a "come" and bringing in the rope. He was a big pup, mostly lab, with big webbed feet. He was a smart pup, but he had no attention span. Everything in the world was important to him, everything was new and had to be investigated.

The air was just starting to go to chill, and there was the faintest odor of woodsmoke on the breeze. Maybe that was a good idea. Maybe he would have a fire. He'd make a shaker of martinis, maybe grill a steak. He and the dog would lounge by the fire. They didn't need her. They'd be fine by themselves.

"Would you like that, boy? Would you like a fire? Some steak? I'm afraid you're still a little young for martinis, but maybe, if you play your cards right, we could swing an olive. How would that be? You want an olive?"

The pup turned tight circles in front of him as he went down, trying to lick his chin at the same time he went over onto his back, paws waving in the air. He bent down and let the pup lick his chin. "That's right. We don't need her. We can have a good time all by ourselves, can't we? She can go out where ever she wants, with whoever she wants. We'll have a good time right here." The pup was squirming hard now, as though he had no spine at all, panting and drooling, thrilled with the attention.

They had had the dog for a little over a month. They had gone together to a house two towns over, answering an ad in the paper. They had paid the young boy there ten dollars for him. He was the smallest of the litter, but active and happy. He and his wife had cooed and tickled the pup, and the pup had squirmed in delight and bit at their fingers.

"What are we going to call him?"

"I don't know."

"Look at his feet, they're huge."

"Francis, then."

"Francis?"

"Francis. He's got big feet."

"Who's Francis?"

"He is." He had put his arm around her while she

held the squirming pup, and he had been happy, as happy as he had been in a long time. Their life with the dog unfolded before him, and they were happy — the way they had been years before.

"Francis," he said, picking up the stick. "Get it." He threw the stick out about twenty feet, letting the dog scramble up and after it. When the dog had the stick in his mouth, having first wrestled with it, then picked it up and begun prancing with it, he said "come," and tugged on the rope. The dog stopped for a minute, then put his head down and charged back toward him.

"Good boy, good boy. Come on, let's go get a martini." He held the rope and started running for the door, the dog coming on at his heels. When they got to the door he praised the dog again and bent down to unhook the rope.

And that suddenly, the dog turned and was gone. He ran down the walkway, shouting. "Francis. Come. Come, boy." And he heard the squeal of the brakes and the thud and yelp just as he somehow knew he would.

When he reached the street, the car had stopped and a man in a hooded sweatshirt and jeans and thick work boots was running back to where the dog writhed on the street. "Oh, God," he repeated. "He just ran right in front of me. Oh, God. I didn't mean to hit your dog."

Francis was down, struggling to get up, but unable to get his hind legs to follow the lead of his front.

"Oh, Jesus," the sweatshirt man said. "You think he's going to be all right?"

He picked the dog up, and it started to yelp again, then bit his hands. "I have to get him to the vet."

"Down the road there. Back on, what is it, Baldwin? There's a vet right there. Take him there."

He drove, talking to the dog who was laid out on the back seat. The dog had stopped whimpering now, and he knew it was in shock.

The vet was just locking up when he got there. "There's nothing I can do," the vet said. "He's going to need X-rays and a trauma room. You're going to have drive him over to Slater. There's a trauma center there. She drew him a crude map and wrote the address. "You better hurry," she said. "He's pretty shocky. But don't kill both of you, now."

People looked at him with wide, sympathetic eyes when he got to the trauma center. One woman, a cat wrapped in a towel on her lap, waved him toward the back room. Only then did he see that his hands and arms were covered with blood.

"We have to do X-rays," the vet, an older man with wire rimmed glasses said. "But first we've got to get him out of shock. It's going to take a while. And I have to tell you, I don't think it looks good. I think we have a spinal cord here. What I want you to do is wash up and go home. When I get him to X-ray, I'll give you a call."

"Whatever time."

The vet nodded. "At whatever time. As soon as I know. And this is hard, but I want to agree right now. If it's spinal, I'm going to put the little guy down. It has to be done. You understand?"

He nodded and the vet nodded back. "Go wash up. Go home, fix a drink, hug your wife, have some dinner. I'll call as soon as I know."

At home, he sat on the couch and drank gin from a tumbler of ice, his hands wrapped in tight layers of gauze. He sat and he drank, and he listened for the phone, or for her foot step on the porch.

Norton did not look that bad. He got behind a couple of batters, but only by one ball, and he was finding the corners. It looked like they had a chance.

At the bar, they were touching now. Little, tentative touches of hand to arm and shoulder.

"I told you that Norton could hang in."

"And I told you both about the couple at the bar. And I want that fifty. The deal is as good as done, here."

He caught the woman looking at him out of the

corner of his eye. When he turned slightly toward her, she looked away, and he did the same. But just a couple of seconds later, he saw her again, but this time he broke his stare before she broke off hers.

He smiled a little to himself. It was a funny thing. He hadn't come in looking for a woman. He wasn't interested, not really. He was after all, married, just out for a drink and a little privacy. He had told himself he just couldn't take one more night sitting in front of the television set, so he'd called his wife, told her he would be late, and stopped in here, where he sat behind a scotch and soda and watched the television over the bar. He had just been thinking that it was about time to get up and go get dinner somewhere.

"You all right, here?" the barmaid asked.

He tapped the rim of his glass with the little plastic straw. "One more, I think. One for her, too." He pointed at her with the straw.

When the barmaid came back, she set his drink down in front of him, then took an orange colored drink down to the other end of the bar. He stared straight ahead for a couple of seconds, then looked quickly to the end of the bar.

The woman held up the orange drink in acknowledgment, nodded and smiled just a bit.

He smiled back. What the hell? What the hell?

He picked up his drink and walked to the end of the bar. He was here for a night of relaxation, a break from the routine. Nothing special. No harm meant. No harm, no foul. A little conversation, then home.

She was younger than he had thought she was, smaller. She looked just a bit drawn around the eyes, as if she hadn't been sleeping well. That was what had thrown him off. He guessed she was nearly thirty. He wasn't yet forty. When he came up right next to her, she extended a thin arm, her hand bent down at a 45-degree angle in what seemed to him an affected gesture. "Laura," she said.

"Glad to meet you, Laura. I'm Vic." He lied.

"Can you believe all that?" she asked.

"Beg your pardon?"

"On the news. Television. You were watching television. Can you believe things like that? Kids. They're just kids, doing terrible things to each other. What's happened to the world, Vic? What is it with kids these days?"

"Terrible," he agreed, though he had not been paying a lot of attention to the news.

"So, Vic. What do you do? For work? What do you do?"

"Construction," he lied again, for no reason he was aware of.

She arched a brow. "These aren't the hands of a construction worker, Vic." The touch of her hand was soft, but oddly discomfiting.

"I haven't touched a hammer in years. I do deals. I hire the crews, put my name on the house when it's done."

"Contractor."

He nodded.

"Give me some help here, Vic. I'm doing all the talking right now."

"Laura. I'm sorry. I'm not much of a talker, I guess. I like to listen. I've liked listening to you, but maybe I'm not such good company." Then, with a vague sense of relief, "I'll go back there, where I was."

"I'm not complaining," she said. "At least, I'm not trying to. Thank you for the drink. I forgot to say that. Do you like music, Vic?"

"Sure. Sure, I like music. Who doesn't?"

"A world full of heartless bastards, Vic." She dug in her purse and pulled out a crumpled dollar bill. "Here, play the jukebox."

He waved off her dollar which seemed tired, wet and shabby. I'll get it. Is there something you'd like to hear, Laura?"

"C-21. That's my favorite song. I'd like to hear that one."

He didn't know most of the songs on the jukebox,

including C-21. He punched that one, starting to punch one he knew, then stopped, embarrassed. He didn't understand what she liked in music. The song he had almost chosen was ten, maybe twelve years old. What if music that he liked seemed ridiculous or old-fashioned to her? He punched a couple at random and then hit C-21 again.

The first song was playing by the time he got back to the bar. Laura had lit a cigarette. She was tapping her cigarette on the lip of the ashtray in time to the music that he didn't recognize. "Thanks," she said.

"You like this song? Me, too. I like this one."

"You like everything he does?" She mentioned a name that he didn't recognize either.

"Pretty much. Not as much as this one, though."

"I like it all. None of my friends do. He stinks. I know that. But I like him. I like him a lot. Funny, huh?" She was swaying slightly to the music. She closed her eyes and took a long drink. Her thin cotton top slid to one side, baring some of her shoulder which was thin and as delicate looking as the wing of a bird. "So, Vic. What're you up to?" She adjusted the strap of her bra, then pulled her top down at the back to straighten it.

The question took him by surprise, as though it were an accusation. He thought maybe it was. "I was thinking maybe we could dance. Do you like to dance, Laura?"

She took another long drink and turned on her bar stool. She set her cigarette down in the ashtray and made a sweeping motion with her arm. "Waltz me."

Her breath was sweet with alcohol and fruit under the cigarette smoke. She turned herself into his body and pulled him tight. He realized for the first time that she was pretty well looped. He put his arm around her, took her other hand and pulled it up close to his face and began a slow turn on the dance floor. She settled right into him, her face on his shoulder so that he could put his nose deep into her hair.

They danced silently until the song ended and

then stayed out on the tiny dance floor while the jukebox brought up the next selection.

The next song was way too fast. It seemed to him nothing but electronic noise with the beat of a pile driver behind it. "You pick this one, Vic?"

He was embarrassed, caught up in his ignorance of music in the last ten years. They stood on the dance floor smiling at each other quizzically. He shrugged. "I didn't think so. Maybe. I must have pushed the wrong button. I don't even know what this is."

Back at the bar, she held on to his hand, until she saw the cigarette still in the ashtray. She dropped his hand and took the last couple of drags off the cigarette.

"So, Laura. What do you do? For work?"

She shook her head sadly. "Everything. Nothing. You name it. I've done it. I've done computers. Waitressed. Bartended. Retail. You name it. Right now I'm enjoying a vacation courtesy of the Republicans. I've got some possibilities, you know? But they're not that much better than unemployment. I've still got a couple more months of that. Terrible, huh? I mean taking unemployment when I could be back working."

"Not so terrible. You earned it. You're not taking their money. You're taking your own money back. What's so bad about that?"

"I've always hated people who did things like that. Now I am one. It's this damned economy."

"Things are tough," he agreed. The loud fast song ended, and the jukebox brought up the first song, again. "I believe we have a dance to finish," he said.

Back on the dance floor, he was amazed at how light and graceful she was. Holding her, he began to have memories of other women, women he had known long before he met the woman he married.

"What are you thinking, Vic?"

"That you feel good in my arms." And he felt good because this was the first thing he had said to her that wasn't some sort of lie.

"So, Vic. You're married, right?"

He felt himself stiffen a little. "No," he said. "I'm not married. Why? Are you?"

"You feel pretty good in my arms, too."

On the way to her place, he drove carefully—a little too slowly. Though he hadn't drunk very much, he felt a little buzzed, a little dazed. When they had first gotten into his car at the bar, they had kissed long and hard, going at each other furiously with their tongues. He had run his hands back and forth across her surprisingly heavy breasts, and he had gotten an erection that made sitting painful. He was still having trouble finding a comfortable position for driving. He felt like he was seventeen again.

When they came into her apartment, still clutching and grabbing at each other, he was immediately struck by the sweetness of the air. It was thick with perfume, and under that, mildew. Over everything was the stale smell of old cigarette smoke. She was kissing the side of his neck, and he was running his hands up the back of her blouse, trying to unhook her bra.

"Wait," she said. "Wait, Vic. I better go pee."

While she was gone, he walked through the little apartment. The furniture was all covered with pieces of fabric that didn't hide the fact that the seat cushions were lumpy, the frames probably sprung. The paneled walls were covered with posters and pictures cut from magazines, all held in place by straight pins.

In the bedroom, the bed was covered with an old chenille bedspread that was going threadbare. The bedroom furniture was all mismatched, old and badly scarred. It was the sort of furniture he assumed you would find at a thrift store. There were more pictures from magazines pinned to the walls. The linoleum of the bedroom floor was covered with worn area rugs. At each side of the bed was a small table covered with cloth. When he accidentally bumped into one, he realized it was a cardboard box. Everything was clean, but it was shabby and poor.

She came into the room. Blushing a little, she tossed her bra onto the dresser. "I thought it was easier if I did it. Those things are always so hard to get unhooked when you're in a hurry. You want something to drink, Vic? I think there's some wine in the fridge."

"No," he said. "No thank you. No wine."

She moved into him, kissing him hard, running her hands up and down the front of his shirt. "Good," she said. "I don't want any, either."

They continued to kiss as they undressed, trying not to break contact as they struggled with their clothes. When they were both finally naked, she took his penis in her hand. "Oops. Not quite ready here." And she kneeled down in front of him.

He put his head back and closed his eyes, working at enjoying this. But he kept opening his eyes, looking at the room around them. It was just too poor, too terrible a way for anyone to live. The dampness and age of everything here seemed oppressive.

"What's wrong, Vic? You want me to do something else? What do you like? What would you like me to do?"

"That's fine," he said. "I like that. You're very good."

"A little slow to come around, huh? Why don't you just lie back on the bed. Just relax. Leave everything to me. Don't worry about anything. I'll do all the work."

Lying on his back, he looked at the water stains on the ceiling, and suddenly this was just all too real for him. He felt terrible, for himself, for his wife, and mostly for Laura. He had a comfortable home miles from here. He couldn't even imagine living like this. He felt he was using Laura, exploiting her poverty, her need. He hadn't meant for things to come to this. The world seemed to him too tattered, too real. He was ashamed. He had picked up this woman in a bar, told her lies, manipulated her. And here she was, a poor woman, obviously struggling just to get by, going down on him, trying to please him. He put his hand on her forehead and gently pushed her away.

"What's the matter?" she said.

He shook his head slowly. He could feel his heart racing. "I'm sorry," he said. "This isn't right. I've done something terrible. I've lied to you. I am married. I'm not a contractor. My name's not even Vic. I'm so sorry. I've been terrible to you. I'm not a bad person. I'm sorry. This is just terrible. I better go."

He got off the bed and began gathering up his clothes. While he dressed, Laura got up from the bed and walked naked to the dresser. She shook a cigarette from her pack and lit it. She let her head fall back and she braced her arms on the dresser.

When he was dressed, he moved a couple of steps closer to her. "Forgive me," he said. "I didn't want to be mean to you. I didn't mean to lie to you, it just happened. I don't do things like this. I'm a decent man. I didn't mean to tell you lies just to get you into bed. I just wanted to talk. This just happened. Forgive me."

She put her cigarette in the ashtray and turned to face him. Her body, despite the heaviness of her breasts, looked pitifully thin and delicate, something easily broken. "Vic," she said. "I knew you were lying. All of it. And, you want me to forgive you, Vic? You know what you are, Vic? You're a selfish bastard."

The last out was a fly to short right field. All three of them clapped and made exaggerated gestures of relief, mopping their brows, fanning themselves. Don and Larry exchanged high fives.

"Glad it's over," Larry said. "But that also means it's time to hit the road. I think we're going out to dinner tonight. I've got to shower and change."

"Yeah, guess that's it."

At the door, they stopped and let the couple at the bar go out in front of them. "Good golf," Larry said. "Good game. Good day. And, now, good night."

Art raised his right hand and rubbed his fingers rapidly across his thumb, the money gesture, nodding to where the couple had been. "And all's right with the world."

Vinson, In Passing

homage á Don

Needless to say, we will all miss Vinson. He was, as others have no doubt mentioned, a pretentious twerp. No one is arguing that. He was bright, witty, and well read. He had an abundance of good taste, and he took a joy in life that he was willing to share. But we forgave all that. And he will be missed. He gave good parties, and we were happy to attend them. At his worst, he was interesting, and he always bought good booze. And there was no conceivable reason for him to go to a hardware store.

Except a picture. Rather, a lithograph. A Jim Dine lithograph. One of those ubiquitous bathrobes. It cost a pretty penny, no doubt. But Vinson had lots of those pretty pennies, and he never minded parting with them. That's another reason Vinson will be missed.

Vinson chose to hang the lithograph himself. One suspects it was a carefully considered decision, because Vinson did not operate on whim. Hence, the hardware store. It was a small hardware store on the upper eighties, suitably shabby for the upper eighties, fitting in by seeming not to fit in.

Vinson liked the hardware store, though he normally had no use for hardware. He especially liked the smell, a *melange* of wood, oil, and paint under a light touch of dust. After a bit of searching, he picked up an eighty-nine cent package of bent hangers, rated at fifty pounds. Vinson tried to imagine what fifty pounds felt like. He couldn't. He reasoned then, that the Dine in a skinny brushed steel frame couldn't possibly weigh fifty pounds.

He felt a vague sense of dread at the possibilities of hanging the print himself, especially the pounding of an actual nail into actual plaster. He had a hammer that was just dandy for cracking ice for Daiquiris and Margaritas, but Vinson was a little unsettled at the thought of actually driving a nail with it. So, Vinson wondered.

There seemed to be enough hardware in the store to take the world apart and reassemble it in some more reasonable, orderly fashion. Vinson, non-mechanical, wouldn't be the one to do that. He considered the irony that those who had the ability to actually rebuild the world, seemed to have no inclination to do it. Probably for the best.

The Weed Eater was at the back of the store among pruning shears, hoses, trowels and window boxes. It was green and awkwardly constructed, its head at an oblique angle to its long, aluminum neck. From the far end of that neck, dangled a ridiculously short cord, no more than eight inches. Vinson considered why a hardware store in the upper west side would carry Weed Eaters. He tried to imagine how anyone could use one only eight inches from an electrical outlet. It was an absurd little machine, and on the whole, he liked it better than the Dine bathrobe.

Vinson hung the Dine midway down the curving foyer of his apartment, close enough to the Chuck Close self portrait that one could take both of them in more or less simultaneously, and across the hall from the Katz and the Pearlstein–one of those hard-edged, objectified nudes that represented no moral dilemmas, but, rather, a kind of comfort in its very unattractiveness. All in all, Vinson had a considerable collection that was not terribly far from museum quality.

In the center of the foyer, facing immediately anyone who walked through the front door, Vinson placed the Weed Eater, resting on top of a yellow plastic, retro table he had picked up in Soho. Next to it, he placed a small white card—Weed Eater; 10" cutting path; 2.8 amps; 4 lbs; aluminum and plastic; American–1999. A nice touch, Vinson thought, for after all, art is necessarily collage.

The arrangement pleased Vinson, and us, too, as we stood around dispensing small chuckles and knowing smiles at Vinson's joke before heading for the bar. We commented on the knowing twinkle in his eye. He was on to something.

"Humor," Vinson said. "Is the basis of all art. One brush stroke laid on differently, and *Guernica* is pure vaudeville."

He had us there. Off we went to the bar and the television and a Rangers' game.

But things progress. Vinson's joke grew slightly stale at the edges. He reinvigorated it for a while by adding a bright blue fourteen-gauge, fifty-foot extension cord that he arranged over the course of three days until he settled on a series of ogees of descending radii, snaking down the hall.

It was, one supposes, only a matter of time until Vinson succumbed and plugged the thing in. In the minutes of low dread between martini two and martini three—and those are moments that we must imagine from this point on—one could see the gleam in Vinson's eye as he finally pushed the trigger and heard for the first time the maddeningly mellifluous shriek of the little machine, something like a vacuum cleaner gone slightly hysterical.

When one is holding a ten-inch Weed Eater, plugged in, trigger engaged, the cutting head spinning a piece of monofilament line at many, many revolutions per second, ready to cut something down, one presumably looks for something to cut. What Vinson had was a 100% wool level-loop carpet in dove gray. He touched the line ever so slightly to the carpet. Close your eyes for a moment and see the little tufts of gray wool bouncing into the air, then floating back to the carpet where the trimmer line catches them again and sends them spinning up once more. A lovely effect, pure Vinson.

Again, the twinkle in Vinson's eye and inquiries from those of us who cared for him.

"Power," Vinson replied.

When the carpet was down to bare backing, a square weave of what looked like packing twine, the result of a process that took nearly a month of concerted effort, Vinson waded in the dove gray dust that covered his apartment, rudderless, a man without purpose. Chuck Close stared at him in dispassionate, rectangular boredom. Vinson looked at the throws—the Dhurries, Kilims, Sarouks, and the one Ganado Red. Handmade and tight, they lasted longer. Vinson went back to the hardware store for more trimmer line.

When there was nothing left in the apartment but the scattered fuzz of a hundred long dead sheep, Vinson went looking for new material. The Weed Eater did nothing to the steel base of the Eames chair, barely scratched the oak of the Stickley bedstead.

Then, quite by accident, while he was trying to make progress on the cherry bookcase, he bumped it. A slim volume fell out. Vinson moved forward, letting the Weed Eater graze the thin, brittle pages, sending up strips of wrinkled, ink-stained paper. In time, he learned how to turn the pages of the book with the head of the Weed Eater and hit the trigger just as the pages came to full upright. In this manner did Vinson finish the *Tractatus Logico Philosophicus*.

The twinkle returned. "Philosophy," Vinson replied.

He moved on. *Decline of the West, Miss Macintosh, My Darling, Glas*, then Barth, Barthelme and Cheever. When he was done, the floor was several inches deep in stained and shredded paper. It was a wonderful effect—visual and kinetic. Carrying our cocktails, we waded through Vinson's apartment, shredded prose crunching under our feet, little mutilated words catching on socks and hose. We congratulated Vinson. It was worthy of Beuys. I pulled a tiny chunk of paper from my cuff and unfolded it like a small accordion—*angui*. "Tranquil?" "Languish?" "Anguish?" Chuck Close remained dour. Vinson twinkled.

"Deconstruction."

The Jim Dine litho went in about a minute. Chuck Close resisted for over an hour, but at the end the effect was simply the natural progression of art in the eighties. Vinson bought an original deKoonig, and acetate cells from *Fantasia* which made a splendid, bright ripping sound.

"Art," Vinson said, "has returned to where it began."

One night, while working on the last of the deKoonig, a shred six inches by seven, on which Vinson still owed twenty-eight thousand dollars, he let the head of the Weed Eater fall, accidentally brushing against his the soft flesh of his bare foot.

It was an immediate and brilliant thrill, raising a bright red welt on his skin that later disintegrated into a thick, sagging slug of dark blood against Vinson's white skin. He put the Weed Eater down and began slowly, methodically, taking off his clothes.

Later, leaning down to Vinson, I wished I were wearing a better tie. I could not help but notice, though, beyond the blood, beyond the tatters of skin like little banners at a used car lot, beyond the shocky glaze, the light in his eye.

Vinson blinked once, coming for a second out of shock or *Nirvana*—perhaps they're the same thing—like a man getting off a Barcalounger.

"Vinson," I said. "Tell what you have found. Now. At last."

Vinson smiled. "Love."

Getting Bud

"Robbie. Robbie wake up." My father's voice cut the heavy mist that surrounded me. I fought against it, trying to curl deeper and deeper inside myself.

"Robbie you have to get up." His large hand shook me and hauled me up from where I had lodged. His face loomed above me, pulled me to him. "We have to go somewhere."

It was summer. I was eight and my father and I were alone while my mother took care of her father in Kentucky. He was dying, though I didn't understand that at the time. I only knew that I spent long hours by myself. Sometimes my father took me to work with him, but mostly he had to leave me home. I read and watched television and tried to stay in out of the Arizona heat.

"You have to get dressed," my father said. He helped me pull my pajamas off. "We have to go out," he said, handing me clothes—my shirt, my jeans and boots.

I don't think I said anything. I didn't understand what we were doing, but I was too sleepy to ask. We were going out and I had to put on my clothes. I understood that much, and that was enough. "Here," he said, handing me a pair of underpants. "Put these on, too."

"Where are we going?" I finally asked, waking up, and understanding that this was something very strange.

"A long way," my father said. "We have to go a long way and get Bud."

Outside, it was dark and cold. I shivered in my thin shirt, though it was the middle of summer. As we walked to the car, my father's DeSoto, I thought I had never known that night could be so quiet.

"What time is it?" I asked.

"It's almost midnight."

"Is Bud all right?"

"I think so. He needs some help getting home, that's all."

Bud was my father's best friend. Or maybe my father was Bud's best friend. He was tall and blonde with hair he slicked back. But he had hair that wouldn't stay put, and there was always a thick shock of hair on his forehead. Bud worked with my dad down at the plant, though they did not work together. Bud worked on the dock and my dad worked in the office.

Bud came to our house nearly every weekend, and often during the middle of the week. I think we ate more dinners with Bud than without him. Sometimes he brought a woman to the house, sometimes not. I liked some of the women he brought, especially Betty, who could pay attention to me without embarrassing me or being goofy. She talked to me and asked real questions and said real things.

Lots of the women he brought were loud and happy. They laughed too much and either hugged and grabbed at me or ignored me all together. Bud had once had a wife, Ann, though I barely remembered her. She had left a few years before and gone back east—to Ohio or Iowa or Illinois. I think I remember that she was nice, but maybe I was only told that. The years between five and eight are very long years.

Bud could throw a football sixty yards and had played football at the very high school I would go to five years later. He loved music that my parents didn't, and he brought records by Elvis Presley and the Everly Brothers and Fabian and Lloyd Price to the house and played them. They were the small 45's, not the big, breakable 78's my parents had. Sometimes he left them so I could play them when my parents were out.

We drove north, out of the city and into the desert. It was all black and white. The moon was full and the desert was lit by a light that bleached everything white, as if it had snowed that night. I felt like I was still asleep.

We stopped at a bar. I had seen it before, passing it on the way from Tucson to Phoenix. The Hanging Tree. It was a long low building with a painting of some low-growing horizontal tree on the side. The tree was like a mesquite drawn by someone who had never seen one, only heard it described.

"I can't leave you in the car," my father said. "You're going to have to come in with me. This is kind of a rough place. You stay right with me. Don't wander off. Don't leave my side. Don't talk to anyone." I could feel the presence of my mother behind his words.

I had been in bars before, but only in the daytime. Walking from the dark into this bar was like walking from night to day or from sleep to waking up. Years later, I would understand the difference between lounges and bars. Lounges are dark and intimate. Bars, real bars where people drink, dance, play pool and find each other are brightly lit and loud. Important things happen in bars.

Most of this bar, and it was huge, was taken up with a dance floor. It was wooden and there must have been a dozen couples dancing on it. There was no band, only a Seeburg jukebox against the far wall. When we walked in Bobby Helms was singing "My Special Angel." It was a song I knew from school and top forty radio. On rainy days, when we couldn't play ball, the boys' and girls' P. E. coaches forced us into the gym and made us dance. I had to dance with Maureen Hobbs to "My Special Angel." She counted with the song, and our hands sweated. With each step we took, I could feel the shock coming up from her ankles and knees through her body. Until then, I had liked her O.K.

I had never thought about adults dancing to the same records that kids in gym class had to dance to. I had seen plenty of adults dancing. My parents had parties several times a year, but then, adults danced to Glenn Miller, Woody Herman and the Dorseys. Here, they were dancing to Bobby Helms and I saw one lady running her hand across her partner's behind. I pretended not to see and hoped my father wouldn't see it either.

We found Bud in a booth toward the back of the bar, behind the pool tables and next to the duckpin machine. He was sitting alone. There was a tall brown bottle of beer in front of him, and he held a white bar towel to the side of his face. The towel was full of ice and had a pink stain on it. Bud was wearing a blue cowboy shirt with big white flowers on it. One sleeve was torn at the shoulder.

"Let's see," my father said.

"Hi, Robbie," Bud said. "How are you doing, buddy?"

"Let's see," my father repeated. And Bud took the towel away from his face. The side of his face was swollen, and his lower lip was cut. His right eye was swelling up. He smiled a crooked smile. "I guess I'm going to have a pretty good shiner, huh, Rob?" He talked directly to me, as if my father were not even there.

"How'd it happen?"

"Tom," he said, as if he saw my father for the first time. "It wasn't much. I'm all right."

"A woman," my father said.

I laughed. I couldn't imagine a woman beating up someone as big and strong as Bud. Bud shrugged.

"Husband?" my father asked. "Boyfriend?" Now I was terribly confused.

"Husband, I suppose," Bud said. "I'm not sure. There wasn't a lot of conversation."

I kept looking at the duckpin machine. The lights were on, but the pins were stuck up. I could see the thick silver puck on the platform of the machine. I kept looking at it. I would force myself to look at Bud and my father, and then I would look back at the machine. When a waitress came over, I got up and went to the machine. I knew better than to ask my dad for a dime, so I just slid the puck back and forth along the machine. I loved the heft of it in my hand—round and hard and smooth. It slid like it was on ice.

"Robbie," my father said.

Back at the table, my father was looking at Bud's hand, holding it with his finger and thumb, pressing his thumb along the top every now and then.

"Son-of-a-bitch," Bud said suddenly, then, "Sorry, Rob."

I was sure he should have been apologizing to my father instead of me. I loved hearing people talk like that.

"Think it's busted, Tom?"

My father shook his head. "I can't tell. I don't think so. Probably ought have it looked at, though."

Bud held his swollen right hand up for me to see. "I got him a good one, Rob. No matter what happens, get your licks in. That's important. Let them know they've been in a fight. It's no crime to lose a fight. I lost of few of them." He laughed. "But you got to get your licks in. Don't ever let someone walk away unhit.

"I'm O.K." he kept saying. My father wasn't saying anything. "Tom," Bud insisted. "I'm all right. I wouldn't even have called you except we came in her car."

The waitress came back and set beers down in front of Bud and my father. It surprised me, since I never saw my father drink beer. At home he drank martinis or a Tom Collins and never very often. She put a ginger-ale in front of me.

"I met her in the Elbow Room, back in town. Hell, I didn't know she was married. We had a few drinks, a couple of laughs. She had a Cadillac convertible. We went for a ride. My God, Tom, what a car."

Past the duckpin machine, a couple had begun playing pool. Both of them were wearing jeans and boots. I never saw that many grown up ladies wearing jeans, except when it was Rodeo week. She saw me staring at her and gave me a smile.

I was wearing a white cowboy shirt. It had a yoke of red piping, and inside the yoke a cactus, six-guns and horses' heads were printed right onto the material. I had jeans held up by a beaded belt. In the back, the beads spelled out "Robbie." There were red arrows on either side of my name, and the belt had been made by real Indians. I was wearing brown cowboy boots that were scuffed at the toe.

"She wasn't even a looker, you know," Bud said. "She was pretty big, but I like a woman with something to hang on to. Hell, Tom, she was fat. I got beat up over a fat girl." And, unbelievably, Bud started to cry. My father leaned over, reached into his pants and pulled out a couple of dimes. He pointed over to the duckpin machine.

I put the first dime in the machine, and lights flashed, bells rang and the little plastic pins came down. Under the pins, small triangles of wire stuck out of the surface of the alley. I had done this enough to know that to win you had to slide the puck not over the center wire, but either of the two next to it, so that it simulated a bowling ball sliding into the pocket. When you did it right, all the pins went up and lights and bells went crazy. "Strike" lit up on the back of the machine. I wasn't good at pinball, but I liked duckpins, and I made several strikes.

The lady who had smiled at me applauded when all the bells rang. She and her partner were standing right behind me now. "He's very good, isn't he, Charlie?"

"Yeah," Charlie said. "He's great."

The lady moved closer to me and pulled me to her. "You're just adorable," she said. I could smell her sweat, her perfume, and the cigarette smoke. My head rested between her breasts, as she pulled me hard into her. Her hand slid up and down my chest and belly. "Isn't he adorable, Charlie?"

"Yeah. Now leave him alone and come back to the table. You're drunk."

She pulled me around and bent down so we were face to face. "You're adorable," she said. "I want you to grow up and be better than Charlie. You're going to break a lot of hearts, kiddo." I could see a lot of her breasts where her shirt was unbuttoned. She gave me a kiss, and I could smell the sweet liquor on her breath. It was nice.

"Of course, I love Ann," Bud was saying when we got back to the table. "I've always loved Ann. She was the first, Tom." And I had no idea what he was talking about. "Robbie," Bud said. "How's your ginger-ale? Let me buy you another one." He held up his sore right hand for the waitress. I could see that his eye was almost swollen shut now. On the jukebox, Elvis Presley was singing "All Shook Up."

"You could call her," my father said.

"I have," Bud said.

"She loves you. You love her," my father said, though he didn't sound like my father. "My God, Bud. It's not that hard."

"But I'm not like you, Tom," Bud said. "You do things right. You and Ellen. . . . It's easy for you." He stopped and pushed the towel full of ice back into his face. It was steadily dripping water onto the table.

"What is it you want, Bud? What are you looking for?"

"What you've got, Tom. Ellen and Rob, here. I want that, too. The thing is, I just can't. I try, Tom. God knows, I've tried."

"Bud, none of it is horizontal, you know." Then my father, looked at me, suddenly. I knew he was trying to figure out whether or not I had understood that remark. I hadn't the foggiest idea. The waitress brought more beer and ginger-ale. Bud wasn't crying anymore, but he wasn't that far from it, either. He looked at me and winked. Both eyes were shut then.

"If he's all right, you might want to take him home," the waitress said. "He didn't make a lot of friends in here tonight."

My father nodded. "I need to get Robbie back to bed," he said. "Ellen would have my hide if she knew I had him here."

Bud nodded and tilted his head back, taking a long suck at the beer bottle.

"Drink your ginger-ale," my father told me.

"Tom," Bud said, "I really try. You've got to believe that. I just don't know how you do it. Honestly. You understand something that I don't."

"The thing is," Bud said, turning to me. His eyes were swollen nearly shut, but it was clear that he was crying. "You may understand this someday, Rob. What we've got is this world where anything can happen, where even fat girls can have great cars. And it's just too wonderful. It's just too damn wonderful."

Las Momias

Mark found the newspaper in *Terminal Norte*, the ten-acre bus station that connected Mexico City with the northern parts of Mexico. It was called *Alarma*. He had been looking for a newspaper in English because his Spanish was halting. *Alarma* was not in English, but he was able to make out some of the headlines. Besides there was a picture of a young girl with a grotesquely hairy face on the cover with the caption, "*Lobita*," the little wolf. He was intrigued.

They were on their way to Guanajuato, which friends had told them was a beautiful town. Picturesque, like a European village in the middle of the Mexican mountains. And there were mummies on display in a museum. He was curious and vaguely excited to see the mummies. His wife said she had no interest, but he thought maybe she really did.

They were not doing well. Alicia had lost her mother a couple of months earlier. She often spent her days working over the details of the estate her mother had left behind. Nights she would awake weeping. Neither of them had understood how consuming death could be. But Alicia had given up much of her life to her mother's death. It was a huge, demanding child that could not be ignored.

A year earlier, Mark had lost his best friend, who had died of cancer. He had hung on for over a year, though he had been given only three months to live. The progress of the disease had been slow and terrible. His friend lived all the way across country, and Mark saw him only a few times, and each time the disease had taken more of him—his strength, his weight, his hair, his sense of humor, his coordination, his interest in anything that was not his death. It was like watching a person being erased.

Neither of them slept well anymore. They drank too much, and they feared their dreams. But fear of dreaming only leads to more drinking. During the day, they longed for sleep. At night, they fought against it.

He came across the picture on page eight of the paper. It was a car, hideously mangled. Nighttime, everything lit in the slick glare of strobe lights. There was a body just a few feet from the open, twisted door of the car. Everything was wrong. The arms and legs were impossibly contorted, perhaps even disconnected. There was no head, only a surprisingly small sheen of blood (perhaps, he thought, they had already started to wash down the scene). In front of the car there was a round, indistinct object that he thought might be the head. He thought of pictures he had seen of the Jayne Mansfield wreck back in the sixties. He could read little of the caption, though it was two policemen, both dead.

"Oh my God, "Alicia said. "Is that his head?"

"I think so."

"Oh Jesus. Why do they need to show that?"

"It's a different culture than ours. They're not embarrassed by death."

"Well, God. Maybe they should be."

They thought they would sleep in Mexico. They had found a charming old hotel with a courtyard and a fountain. Everywhere ceramic tile glistened in the sun, and there was a bar that would bring drinks up to the rooftop balcony where they sat and took the sun when they were tired of walking and shopping.

The hotel had once been a convent, but there was no indication of that other than a line in a travel book they had brought with them. But neither of them slept at night, no matter how much alcohol they poured into themselves. They would fall asleep in the early morning only to be awakened by the bells of the cathedral across the *truco*. Mornings, they would sit across from each other in the restaurant, drinking *café American* and complain.

"I think it's an excess of faith," Alicia said.

"Or an excess of virginity."

"Don't start."

Jennifer was helping Duncan to walk. Though it was not yet noon, he was already drunk. They were searching for a bar they had heard about back at S.M.U., a bar in a basement somewhere in the narrow streets of Guanajuato. The specialty of the bar was watermelon, soaked in vodka. They served huge chunks of it, that you ate with your hands, getting drunker and drunker as you chewed the sweet fruit. Duncan had become obsessed with it, and they had already been to six bars, looking for the vodka watermelon.

The rest of the group was still in San Miguel de Allende. Jennifer and Duncan had snuck out at breakfast and taken the bus to Guanajuato where the rest of the group would come in two days, but only stay for one night. Duncan was afraid that one night would not be enough to find the hidden bar.

The group was a Spanish class from S.M.U. They were earning three hours of credit for a two week tour of Mexico that was costing their parents thousands of dollars. Jennifer's father, who was a banker in Beaumont, protested that it would be cheaper to take a regular tour. But then there is no credit, Jennifer explained. She was not sure now that there would be any credit since they had ditched the group and would not reconnect for two days.

They would do the work, Duncan explained. They would look up León and Delores Hidalgo on the internet, and they would write the reports they were required to submit. They could do as much on their own as with the group. Their Spanish was very good. Duncan got B's without studying. Jennifer studied hard, and sometimes she got B's as well, but mostly A's. They both thought the group and the middle aged Spanish professor and her husband, who was a physics professor at a Dallas community college, were goofy. Jennifer didn't care about the watermelon, but she liked Duncan, and she liked sleeping with him when he wasn't sick drunk.

They were in a small shop in one of the tiny *trucos*, alleys, that came off the main streets. They each had an armful of souvenirs—ceramics, weavings and carvings. She was looking at a small *retablo* of two *calaveras*— skeletons—playing pool. The *calaveras* were dressed in tuxedos and held burning cigarettes in their teeth. The balls they were playing were skulls. "*Mira*," she said. It was one of the few Spanish expressions they knew and used—*mira*, "look."

"That's great," he said. Mark was a little drunk. They had discovered Havana Club Rum from Cuba and had been drinking it at every opportunity. And he had smoked a *Partaga* on the patio of the restaurant as they drank, though he had not smoked in a couple of years, enjoying it mostly because it was Cuban and forbidden in the United States. And now he was lightheaded and happy. Alicia was seeming to hold her liquor better than he did these days.

"What's it mean?" she asked.

"It's like the inevitability of death, the familiarity of it. Or like a *momento mori*. I don't know."

"You could have just said you didn't know."

"I did. Eventually."

She held it up so the young shopkeeper could see it. "*Calaveras*," the shopkeeper said.

"Sí, But, what does it mean?"

The shopkeeper smiled broadly. "*Perdón*?"

"What is it for? What is it about?"

The shop keeper gave a look of recognition. She shrugged and laughed. "*Mexicanos*," she said, as if that explained everything.

Duncan was sick again, but functional. "You should have switched to coffee, like I did," Jennifer told him.

"Do you know what it's like to puke coffee? It's the worst. It's worse than anything else I know. If you're going to drink, you've got to keep at it."

Jennifer considered telling him that she had switched, and she felt fine, but she didn't. It would only make him angry, and that would make his headache worse. Besides, he was proud of his ability to drink, and she knew better than to point out that she rarely made herself sick, and never as much as Duncan.

They were waiting at their hotel for Francisco, a guide recommended by the desk clerk. He was going to take them to Delores Hidalgo, to see the cathedral and to eat the famous ice creams of Delores Hidalgo — avocado, corn, and shrimp, among others. She thought that this was a bad idea for Duncan, but he had been told that the watermelon bar had once been in Guanajuato, but had moved to Delores Hidalgo.

"We are coming up to a cemetery where one of Delores Hidalgo's most famous citizens was buried. This man was a star of many films in Mexico and the writer of over four hunret songs. He was the most famous man from Delores Hidalgo except for Father Hidalgo himself, the great hero of the revolution. He is buried in a most wonderful grave that was designed by his son.

"After his death he came back to Delores Hidalgo as he had said many times he would. In his death he had done great honor to this town that we are about to visit.

"It is most unfortunate. It is an accident, I think." They looked ahead from the backseat of the car. There was a line of cars, and there were flashing lights from emergency vehicles. "Many people die on this road, though the road is a very good one."

They had come down the highway between Guanajuato and Delores Hidalgo very fast. Their guide had passed slower cars without concern, often without good sight lines ahead. They had sat in the back seat and had held each others' hands tightly. The guide drove with one hand and told stories as their tires had squealed through the curves. Once they were on the flat, he had accelerated more. Neither of them looked at the speedometer, because they did not want to know.

"It is all right," Francisco said. "We will just go arount. The cemetery is just ahead." A policeman raised a hand to halt them, then waved them on past on the shoulder of the road to the area in front of the *cemetario*. "Oh," he said. "Now I understand. It is the funeral of two policemen who were killed on this road last week. It was a terrible accident."

"What happened?"

"A terrible thing. It was late at night and the two policemen were on their way home from Guanajuato where they had business. It had rained. The one who was driving fell asleep. They drove into the back of a truck that was going very slow. It was a terrible thing."

"Was this in the newspaper?"

"It was a terrible thing. Newspapers always want to show terrible things. It helps people understant that their lives are not so terrible as they think."

They got out of the car and walked toward the front gate of the *cemetario*. Cars were parked helter skelter around the cemetery. Now two hearses made their slow way toward the gates where they had stopped and stepped back against the wall out of respect. There were people all around them, many of them uniformed police. There was a variety of uniforms, and they had no idea of what the uniforms represented.

When the hearses had stopped, a pickup truck pulled up along side it, and musicians climbed out of the bed, carrying trumpets, a tuba, trombones and drums. They scrambled into a kind of order in front of the hearses. Now another pickup truck came up. In the back were huge arrangements of leaves and a few flowers. They were constructed on heavy wooden frames and two men took each one.

The musicians began a slow march, a dirge. And they led the mourners in through the gate. Two boys followed holding banners aloft. Then came the two caskets, borne by policemen. The families, dressed in black, the women, veiled, followed. Behind them came the enormous arrangements of greenery.

Then the crowd of people surged and they were caught up in it. Duncan bumped into an enormous policeman who mumbled, *"Perdón."* It was starting to freak Duncan. He was hung over, and he didn't like cops much. They moved with the crowd through the gates and into the *cemetario.* Everything was white. The cemetery was made up of tombs and sepulchers of concrete, washed dazzlingly white. The dirge grew louder as the sound echoed from the walls and off the sides of the tombs. The crowd of mourners formed a thick line, winding its way toward the back of the cemetery. Duncan felt that he was wrapped in the crowd of mourners, who were then wrapped in the thick, soft music. They pulled him along, away from Jennifer. He was marching with the policemen toward the back of the *cemetario* to bury the other two policemen. The dirge became the rhythm of his walk, the rhythm of his heart.

He felt a pull on his sleeve, and saw Francisco, pulling him from the line over to where Jennifer waited for him. He turned and watched the procession file past him. There must have been a couple of hundred people, all moving toward the back of the cemetery where he could still hear the band playing another slow march.

"This is the grave. It was built here to celebrate the wonderful life of this man who was a great artist."

Francisco motioned toward an enormous structure of low walls built of concrete, embedded with bits of glass and tile. The walls, slowly gaining height, swept toward a huge concrete *sombrero*. The sombrero sheltered a smooth floor of tile that covered the grave itself. "All of these tiles have been made especially for this grave," Francisco said. "Each one contains the title of one of his many songs."

"Four hundred," Jennifer said.

"That's right. Four hunret songs. This was a very great man."

"This is an enormous cemetery."

Francisco shrugged. "I will tell you about this place. For many years, in this town, was much leather work. And each of the workers carried with him his small, sharp knife. And sometimes after work, they would drink. And when two men drink, it often goes like this. After one, it is 'you are my frien.' And after two, 'you are my brother,' and after three, 'I am your father.' And then out come the knives. And the arguments they end here." He waved his arm around the *cemetario*. "But then, everything ends here. It is all the same. *La vida no vale nada.*"

"Life is worth nothing," Duncan said.

"Yes. Very good. You know Spanish. You study hard. You are a good boy."

That night, Duncan fell asleep early, only to be jolted awake from a nightmare. They were on the road between Guanajuato and Delores Hidalgo, going very fast, completely out of control. He awoke sweating, Jennifer rubbing his arm, calming him. The dream was only a slight exaggeration of the trip, earlier in the day.

Over the year, Mark had come from deep grief into a kind of sweet sadness, losing much of his image of Paul's death, and remembering more of his life. He thought that Alicia would come to this, too, though he knew it would take her longer. Her father had left years earlier, and she had little recollection of or interest in him. She had come untethered now, without her mother. She felt as though she were wandering through her days attached to nothing but the monotony of business and probate. Mark thought, more and more often, that he wasn't strong enough to tether her to himself. They orbited each other like satellites, with no visible connection to each other.

Neither of them slept well anymore. He had a dream in which his friend, Paul, sat down beside him with a beer and said, "And then, next thing I know, I'm dead. What was I thinking? Nothing, obviously." He had tried to tell Alicia the dream, thinking there was some comfort in it, but he had given up.

They waited outside their hotel for Francisco, the guide who would take them around Guanajuato for the sights–the opera house, the statue of La Papilla, who had burned the *granario* during the revolution, and to the *Museo de las Momias*. Francisco swung up the sidewalk on his game leg, full of apologies. "There is another couple," he said. "They are also Americans. Very young. You will like them, I think. Besides, now it will not cost you so much, because they pay also."

They were kids, the other couple. College kids in baggy clothes. The girl was shy and almost attractive, though she had a diamond on the side of her nostril and several small silver rings through her eyebrows. The boy was sullen and had a terrible hair cut, though Mark thought he had probably paid a lot for it. The young people mumbled hellos and crawled into the front seat with Francisco so that Mark and Alicia could sit in the back. Alicia thought they were kind of sweet, but she felt very old.

"Here you will see one hunret mummies," their driver said, dropping them off in front of the *Museo de las Momias*. "One hunret," he emphasized. "Here you will pay your admission, and for me also, as I will explain to you about these mummies. And you will pay extra, only a little, if you want to take pictures, which I think you do."

Inside the rooms were lined with glass cases, coffins, in fact. In each case, a corpse, remarkably intact, the skin dry as paper, in colors from buckskin to copper.

"There is very little room here for to bury people," their guide explained. "So you must rent the grave for seven years. If the rent is not paid for the next seven years, the body is dug up and the grave is rented for someone else. One in every hunret times, they dig up the body and find that the minerals of the earth of these mountains have made mummies. It is these mummies that you see here before you."

The bodies were twisted and contorted, but often fully dressed, one man in a suit, another woman in a negligee. They all shared the grimace of death. "Do not be alarmed because they seem to be screaming," the guide explained. "When you die, the muscles that hold up your jaw fall away and your mouth comes then open. It is always the same. They did not scream, though it looks that way."

They worked their way through the exhibit, stopping at each case. The leathery skin of the mummies became less bizarre, and at each mummy, they stopped longer, studying the faces, which though most had lost their noses, looked remarkably intact. The faces began to take on personalities. Years later they would see the mummies during the opening credits of Wim Wenders' *Nosferatu*. Though the images of the mummies were designed to frighten, they found them charming, like old friends. "*Mira*. It's *Las Momias*."

One mummy, displayed upright, was of a large woman whose hands were held up, flattened against her cheek. "This one," the guide said, "was found that way, upside down in her coffin. She had been buried alive." They continued to stare. How do you wake up, find you are buried alive and then turn over and go to sleep, using your hands as a pillow?

Duncan and Mark stood in front of a mummy whose suit was still intact, though it hung off of him now. He seemed to be shouting something to someone.

"This is really gross," Duncan said. "I mean what's the big deal?"

"It's a *momento mori*, I think," Mark said. "I'm pretty sure that's the attraction. Everything leads to death."

"That's part of it," Duncan said. "But there's more. Way back, the Aztecs believed in an afterlife, and the more horrible your death, the better deal you got in the afterlife. They have this innate interest in grotesque death. They used to cut people's hearts out. And then there's the whole Catholic thing. The saints and the martyrs and the blood of the lamb. It's like Mexico. Life, death, it's all the same. *La vida no vale nada*. Life has no value. You haven't found a bar where they serve watermelon soaked in vodka, have you?"

"No," Mark said. "Thank God."

He went off to find Alicia, who was standing with Jennifer in front of a case of mummified babies. One was in a sitting position, its mouth open as if it were crying. There were pictures of it all over Guanajuato. It was the littlest mummy, though there were plenty of other babies and small children in the display case.

"This is very famous," Francisco said. "A very small mummy. It is like the mascot of our town."

"Let's get out of here," Duncan said. "I've seen about as many dead people as I need to."

"Do you all want to go?" Francisco asked hopefully.

"No," Alicia said. "I want to stay for a while."

"There's a bar just down the street. I saw it when we passed. Maybe it's the one."

"You want to go with them? Have a drink before we leave?" Mark asked.

"No. Go if you want. I want to see the rest of them."

Jennifer shrugged. "Gotta go. Maybe this is the one, you know."

They watched them leave, Francisco trailing along, telling them about the burial customs of Guanajuato. Mark put his hands on Alicia's shoulders, and she leaned back into him. "Kids," he said. "They should learn from this. Bad clothes can last forever."

"Ummmm."

Back in Mexico City, they sat at the Piano Bar across from their hotel. She was drinking Havana Club and he was drinking a terrible Martini, with way too much vermouth. The bar had become a favorite place, though the drinks were expensive and not as good as you could get across the street at the hotel. Around the bar were hunting trophies—heads of goats, deer, and a stuffed bobcat. Various rifles were hung on the walls. A television showed a recorded concert—Rod Stewart, and the sound system belted out Tina Turner. Occasionally they would fall into sync, and the effect was doubly bizarre. There was a piano, but no one played it.

A few drinks later, they went back to their hotel and ate in the small café that faced the street and the Piano Bar. They ate light, preparing to fly home in the morning. They had soup, and giant *coctels de camarone*—parfait glasses stuffed with boiled shrimp, layered with a salsa, heavy with cilantro and *jalapeños*. Across the street a crowd had gathered. They called over their waiter and asked what had happened.

"The piano player," he said. "From the bar, there. He had a heart attack." They continued to eat, watching the crowd expand and contract. The *Cruz Roja* arrived, and there was a great deal of scurrying around, but they could not see anything. When they were done with the meal, they asked their waiter if the piano player was going to be all right. The waiter looked at them quizzically. He pointed to his chest. "A heart attack," he said. "He is dead." He said this as if they understood nothing.

Later that night, when they were done packing,

they turned off the television, having given up both the need and the pretense that they were working on their Spanish, and opened the window for some air. It had begun to rain, a light drizzle. The lights along the street looked smeary and small. From across the street, they could hear a woman weeping on the street where the piano player had fallen. But they left the window open, and her weeping continued after they had both fallen asleep.

News at Sunrise

During the day, men move the river. At night the arc lights of the news crews flare against the river in its new location, banked in concrete, reflecting a broken moon. This is the future of Providence. A bold and ambitious undertaking, says Kay Summers, Newswatch 10, her mouth a taut bow, her teeth perfect. A wind blows up from the river, lifting her hair, the color of a match just lit.

Where I Live

Is the Capital. Whatever was there is torn up and replaced. I live on the wrong side of the river, where thin boys prowl the streets and machines move the earth that moves the river. I live in the third floor of a two-story building. A simple life. There are no windows, nothing on the floor except a pile of bills from Filene's. There is no furniture. I own only a 32-inch Sony Trinitron. It is chained to the wall. Six-gauge chain on ten-inch lag bolts to the studs. The heads of the bolts hammered as round as the moon. When you and I are long gone, the television stays.

While the river is moved, thin boys plot. I have returned home to find more of me missing. A Toyota Corolla, 1985, two televisions, a radio, a tape recorder, a Martin D-18, a Sherwood amplifier, a Radio Shack C. D. player and fourteen C. D.'s, a sleeping bag, one down parka, Mr. Coffee, a Proctor Silex toaster. I wear all my clothes. I buy the other t.v. on time. The Sony Trinitron 32 inch, from Filene's. Then chain and bolts. The bills pile up.

News at Noon

Last year in Providence, there were nineteen murders. One hundred and sixteen rapes. Six hundred and six robberies and six hundred and one assaults. There were four thousand, one hundred and sixty five burglaries. Six thousand, two hundred and ninety five cases of larceny. Four thousand, six hundred and eighty five cases of malicious mischief. Kay Summers, Newswatch 10. Her eyes squint against the fall sun. She pulls her coat closer to her in a gesture of grace and need.

How I Live

I watch the news—sunrise, noon, six and eleven. I work only to survive, and I survive to watch the News. Kay Summers, Newswatch 10. Work is only a way to eat. Eating is the way to build blood. At Travellers' Aid on Union Street, the Street Sheet lists the free lunches. Mostly it is bread and stale. Before dawn at the Dunkin' Donuts at Weybosset, the Ford F150's, the Chevy C10's begin to circle. "I got a construction site to clean. Who wants work?" You can pay the rent and eat while your body builds new blood. And you can watch the News. Afternoons you can go to where the news is likely. The State House, the District Court, Federal Court, City Hall. News vans and satellite dishes. Remote feeds. She is shorter than you might think, but her phrases are elegant. Around the corner from Traveller's Aid, you can sell blood. Once every two weeks. The rest of the time, your body turns stale bread into new blood, and blood buys news.

News At Six

At the Thurbers Avenue overpass, the news vans are gathered like flies on a corpse. I fight my way through them. Kay Summers, Newswatch 10 in parka and cap. Everywhere the lights, obscuring a clouded moon. "It has been snowing for nearly an hour now. It will likely snow through the rush hour. Traffic, as you can see, is moving." Down below, cars drive past, the drivers trying to get home to see the snow on television, to hear their lives from the mouth of Kay Summers.

What I Live For

Constancy love and devotion. Kay Summers does not report these. I would have her know faith and passion. I do not know who first said, "you are so beautiful, you should do the news." True, she is a woman of grace and elegance. I study her mouth as she repeats the vocabulary of news, "extortion," "fraud," "conspiracy," "collusion," "indict," "confess," "stab," "assault," "rape" and "murder." I cannot pretend to understand her fascination with the halt and the lame, the wretched and strange, misery and oddity, the clownish and dull. But her words ignite me, and I spend my nights burning in the pure flame of the news.

News at Eleven

They pile wood in tiny cages, light it and send the light down the river. It is a bit of strangeness in the summer night. Crowds line the river, pointing at the fire and water, reflecting a fractured moon. They point and moan. This is news, and they are part of it. Kay Summers winds up the broadcast, and pushes her way through the crowd. She passes in front of me. I reach out to touch her and catch my breath. I cannot let go. I cannot let go.

Quantrill

Alaska, 1904

The storm had started up an hour before. The bar had been filling since morning in anticipation of weather that was coming in hard and fast. There were nine of them altogether. Some knew each other, regulars—trappers and farmers who used the bar as a central point for meeting and leaving messages. The others were wanderers, travelers, idlers and drifters, pushed here by the first winds of the storm.

The old man had been here since just before noon. He said little. He bought bread, cheese and eggs along with a bottle of brandy and had eaten them alone, in the corner, wrapping his arms around his food as he ate, like a man who, used to the presence of others, did not trust others. He also took a pitcher of water and a glass. He drank slowly, mixing his brandy with a good amount of water, almost more water than a man might want in his drink if it were late afternoon and a hard storm setting in.

Ohio 1846

He was a delicate boy and blond. Handsome. More, pretty. Blue eyes and long curling lashes. Pants, belted at the knee and stockings of white combed cotton, patent-leather shoes. He would break a few hearts one day.

He seemed out of place in the field where the cattle grazed among walnut and hickory trees, picking the last of the deadfall from the autumn crop. He moved carefully from tree to tree, keeping out of sight. He watched where he put his tiny feet. He stepped in neither mud nor muffin, stick nor rill of stale water. He made no sound, and his shoes shone in the morning sun.

From around the trunk of the hickory, he watched a Jersey, udder heavy, snuffing through the mud for the hickories, nearly rotten now, spilled from the petaled husks, the meat going just stale and dry. She pushed with her broad flat nose, moving the nuts deeper into the mud, forcing her to work harder for them. Beyond her, thirty yards to the fence and safety. When she looked up, he pulled back behind the tree and retied the ribbons on his hat so that his hat would hang behind his neck and not fall.

When she pushed her head down again, snorting and snuffing the mud below, he moved from around the tree and came at her at a dead run. She looked up, startled, a little boy in green, coming at her, the curved blade of the tanning knife just catching the glint of the late morning sun. She tensed to move at shoulder and haunch, her legs flexing down, preparing to wheel away toward the center of the field beyond the little green boy.

How long it took her to feel the knife separating the skin, exposing the gleaming fat beneath it, we cannot know. She was running now, bellowing, her side spraying blood as she moved across the field away from the fire of pain that held her, slobbering, her full udder swinging under her like a sack of grain, nearly tangling her hind legs and sending her to the ground.

On the fence, thirty yards away, the little boy watched and laughed and clapped in the late morning sun.

Alaska 1904

Bill Watson, who owned a few hundred acres just

to the west, took note of the old man and tried to catch him in conversation. In storms like this one, men thrown together for the length of the storm in a one room bar, restaurant, stable, post office and outlet of general merchandise, do not remain strangers very long. He spoke of the storm, though neither he nor the old man had any particular information to share. "It looks to be a bad one," Bill Watson said.

"It seems to me, they don't come any other variety up here," the old man said.

Bill Watson agreed. It was a bad spot for storms.

"Bill Watson."

"Charley Hart."

"Pleased to make your acquaintance."

"The same."

Ohio 1846

"My man seen him do it, just as big as you please. He run up on that Jersey cow and slashed her haunch to shoulder. Then he done sat and laughed on it."

"I'm sorry."

"Sorry won't cut it. Not this time. My man done tarred up the slash, but if she don't take a fester and seize up, her hide is useless come slaughter and I'm out a extra two dollar."

He counted out two dollars, his last, and put it in Simmons' hand. "If she don't make it, I'll take care of the rest as well. I ain't sure how, but I will. You know I'm good for it."

"I do know that. You are most of a good man. But that little one of yours, that little Willy is mean as the devil hisself."

"I don't know what to do. When I go home, I'll beat holy hell out of him, but I'll tell you right now, it won't do a damn bit of good."

Ohio, 1853

Only a year before, William Quantrill had sat where those seventeen students sat, hunched over their slates, laboring over cyphers and letters that should have presented no challenge for students a third their ages. Over the screech and scuff of chalk, the rustling of paper, the hawking back of mucus, he thought he heard the hooves of horses in the distance. When he went to the window, there was nothing, nothing but the long grass of Ohio, disappearing into the distant trees.

He turned when he heard commotion. He saw that Oliver Samuels had taken the lard bucket that contained the Johnson boy's lunch. The Johnson boy was making a futile attempt to take it back, keeping a wary eye on Samuels, who swatted away the boy's attempts as he would a fly.

He took the three steps over to the boys, took the lunch bucket from Samuels and returned it to Johnson. He gave Samuels a hard backhand across the face. The sound of the slap caused one of the girls to utter a shrill peep. Samuel's face went immediately red, and he knew by the sting in his hand how much Samuel's face must hurt.

Oliver Samuels did nothing but blink twice and go back to laboriously scratching numbers on his slate. The numbers, he knew, meant nothing. Numbers were just numbers to Samuels, and he would depend his whole life on the honesty and fear of others. He was a big boy, nearly six feet, the same as William, but he weighed maybe another fifty pounds more and he was more heavily muscled than a bargeman. He was little more than an idiot, but William had seen him slaughtering pigs, picking them up from the ground with one hand grabbing an ear while the other brought a two-pound hammer down hard between the eyes. It was repetitive, efficient and quick, untroubled by thought, and it gave William some affection for the boy.

Alaska, 1904

"What is it that you do, Charley Hart?"

"This and that. More of this and less of that. I move around. I take note of what others do."

"You don't have the gold or the oil fever, then?"

"I am too old for fevers, and I don't dig at the ground. But if others do, sometimes I might be convinced to become a partner."

"So you're looking for partners, then? You're interested in men that might have a promising piece of land and more ambition than money?"

"I am not a fool, and I do not give my money to fools, either."

"There is no need for offence, old friend."

The old man took more brandy and water. "There is never a need for offence. It is like the wind. It comes and goes as it pleases."

Kansas, 1860

William Clarke Quantrill, having left teaching, looking for a new line of work under the name Charlie Hart, failed as a horse thief in Lawrence, Kansas. He was run off by three different farmers and by a band of Delaware Indians. When he tried to sell three stolen horses to a sheriff's deputy, he escaped only by betraying his two partners.

There was more money and less risk in recapturing escaped slaves who made their way north through Lawrence. At this, he became successful, counting on anti-abolitionists to show him the whereabouts of the slaves. The sheriff of Lawrence warned him that if he ever caught Hart with an escaped slave, he would have him hanged.

Kansas, November 1862

Quantrill

There have been fugitive reports circulated, for some weeks, that Quantrill, the notorious predatory chieftain of the border rebels, was making serious preparations to give Lawrence a call. . . . Were it not for . . . the probable loss of valuable lives, we should be inclined to favor Quantrill's purposes against Lawrence, for with any such force as he has yet been at the head of, we are quite well satisfied that to lead it to an assault on Lawrence would be the most fortunate thing that could happen for the future peace of the border. . . . Mr. Quantrill's reception would be warm, should he venture up this way.

> *Kansas State Journal*
> Lawrence, November 6, 1863

Kansas, 1860

Hunting slaves proved profitable for Quantrill, and he gathered to himself a band of ne'er-do-wells, petty thieves, secessionists, sympathizers, horse thieves, wastrels, blood drinkers and cutthroats who rode with him. They included "Bloody" Bill Anderson, Archie Clements, George Todd, Coleman Younger and the James brothers, Frank and Jesse. When war broke out, they called themselves "guerillas" and night riders for the south. Their principal business of capturing escaped slaves and returning them south for the rewards was augmented by bank robbery, rustling and arson.

Kansas, Sept 1862

KANSAS INVADED!
OLATHE SACKED!

QUANTRILL AT WORK!

The town of Olathe . . . was visited and plundered, on last Saturday night, by the secessionists from Missouri, under the lead of Quantrill. Had there been a well organized and drilled company of fifty men in Olathe, the proper guard out, the town could never have been taken. . . . Let other towns take warning. The success of this raid will encourage similar ones on a bolder scale.

Lawrence Republican
Lawrence, Kansas, Sept 11, 1862.

Alaska, 1904

It had grown colder with the dark, and the wind, or at least the sound of it, had picked up. They moved closer together in the small store, the eight of them, though they probably did not realize that they had come closer. The lamps had been lit, and the stove was fed often.

"I don't believe I will ever complain of the heat again," one of them said.

"No," another answered. "It's hellish cold. It makes me homesick for Kansas."

The old man raised his head now and looked around as though he had fallen asleep in the quiet of the evening. "Kansas," he said. "You would be homesick for Kansas?"

"Well, once I thought that unlikely, but this Alaskan spring has given me to reconsider."

"I would never think fondly on Kansas or drink with a man who would."

"Be careful there, old man. I'm not truly fond of the place myself, but my father and both my brothers would live no where else."

"Then they, sir, are curs."

Kansas, August, 1863

General Order Number Ten, issued by Brigadier General Thomas Ewing, commander of the District of the Border, authorized union troops headquartered in the free state of Kansas to cross the border into western Missouri to forcibly remove and exile the suspected families and friends of "bushwhackers," who were raiding eastern Kansas nearly daily. Over one hundred men, women and children were forced from their homes and sent to union prison camps.

"Destroy, devastate, desolate. This is war."
—Senator James Henry Lane, Kansas.

Alaska, 1904

"I would not, old man, speak ill of another's family."

"All those from Kansas are curs and should be shot."

"You are finding yourself some terrible trouble here."

"I'm afraid of no man from Kansas. And all of Kansas are afraid of me." He rose from his table now. He was very drunk and unsteady on his feet.

"Be careful there, Charley Hart. You are not in your right mind at this moment."

"My name is not Charley Hart. I only travel under the name. My name is known to those from Kansas." He swept his arm toward the Kansas men. "My name. My real name is William Clarke Quantrill."

"Charley Hart, you are drunk, and that is not a good joke. Quantrill is over 40 years dead, and the world a better place for all men, Kansas or not."

"I stand before you now. I am not dead, and I am the living man, William Quantrill, the scourge of Kansas."

The drunker he got, the more insistent the old man

became that he was Quantrill. He did not die in Kentucky in 1865 as it was reported. That was someone else who bore a resemblance and, dying, was willing to impersonate Quantrill so that he might escape. He had over the next thirty nine years, worked his way across the country to the west coast as a watchman, a reporter, a secretary to a banker and as a school teacher. Now he had come to Alaska, where there was more opportunity than ever he had seen before.

In the early morning, the old man fell asleep, the storm had subsided into a slow, steady snow. One of the Kansas men motioned to the other. They rose, grabbed the old man and left out the front door, saying, "no one needs to speak of this."

Lawrence, Kansas, August 21, 1863

The column of riders paused at the outskirts of Lawrence, Kansas, while two lone riders made their way through the town. It was nearly dawn now, and the streets were deserted. The air was still cold from the depths of night, but the sky was clear, and it would be hot later on. The two riders returned to the column of 400 men and reported that no preparations had been made against their arrival.

Jo, the dim boy who did odd jobs, was trying to lure a stray cat out from under the stairs of the Eldridge Hotel. He was supposed to be bringing in firewood for the kitchen stoves, but he was fond of cats, and, usually, they were fond of him. He knelt and peered under the stairs where the cat backed further away from him. When he heard the first pops of the guns, he thought it might again be the fourth of July, which would explain why the cat was so spooked, and it would mean that people would be having fun in the middle of town and that they would give him good things to eat. He liked watermelon almost as much as he liked cats.

The reverend Samuel Snyder was dressed only in

his trousers and undershirt and shoes. He had just milked the cow and was toting the bucket back to the house so that they might have breakfast before he went off to see to his company of black Union recruits who were camped about a half mile up the road, across the street from the encampment of the white recruits.

He turned when he heard the horses, nearly spilling the milk that was sloshing in the bucket as he walked. A line of horsemen, probably Union troops, were coming up the road fast. He went to the fence to watch them go by. The first bullet spun him around, sending the bucket of milk across the hydrangeas. The rest of the bullets kept spinning him until he fell to the ground, drenched in his own blood.

It took the riders another three minutes to reach the encampment of recruits, just up the road. Many of the recruits were still asleep, though some had heard the sounds of the horses and the report of the revolvers and were struggling to get into their clothes. Ebeneezer Scott was just buttoning his fly when one bullet passed through his right hand and out his left buttock. Before he had time to cry out, another had torn away the front of his throat.

Ralph Stone and Michael Franks, bunkies, stumbled out of their tent bare naked and were hit with over eight shots apiece. Neither knew what was happening. Within two and a half minutes, all forty-eight of the recruits, black and white, were dead.

The column split into three, and the middle and largest column followed Quantrill to the Eldridge Hotel, the biggest, grandest building in Lawrence. They surrounded the building as the other two columns reattached to the central column. The shooting was random, and the state provost marshal, who was quartered in the hotel, surrendered it to Quantrill, who had worn a tasseled hat with gold braid for the occasion, and was thought, by many of the guests, to be an exceptionally fine looking man.

Jo, the dim boy, who had now been scratched by

the cat, thought to get a better look at what was going on at the front of the hotel. He walked around the southeast corner of the building and skinned up the fence. He saw riders whirling and running in random fashion before his head, the only part of him over the fence, was blown apart.

Inside the hotel, Quantrill made his command post. He had more chairs brought to the lobby for the comfort of the lady guests. He bowed and kissed hands and assured them that whatever else might happen, there would be no lady harmed in any way on this day.

Senator James Henry Lane, who had lobbied for the General Orders against the Missouri bushwhackers, was awakened by a negro, running down the streets, screaming that the bushwhackers had come. Still in his night shirt, the senator jumped from his bedroom window, onto the roof of the shed house and down to the ground. Barefoot, he ran and did not turn to look back.

Lester Sprylock, a drummer from Nebraska, stood in a line in the lobby of the Eldridge Hotel to give up his money and his valuables. When he asked one of the raiders if he might keep a quarter in order to buy a drink at the bar, the raider leveled a Navy Colt .44 to his face, resting the barrel on the bridge of his nose. Deliberately, he drew back the hammer until the revolver cocked. The raider and Sprylock stared at each other over the gun, neither saying a word until the raider began to laugh. The raider lowered the hammer of the pistol and gave Sprylock two dollars, saying, "Before this day is done, I think you may need more than one drink."

Levi Gates, who was known to be the best shot in Lawrence, rode to the outskirts of town, and then readied his hunting rifle. He fired once, and a bushwhacker fell from his horse, a hundred yards away. He ran to the woods and reloaded, fired and killed another bushwhacker. When he turned to run back to the woods, another bushwhacker hit him in the face with the butt of his rifle. The bushwhacker then went on hitting Levi Gates so hard and often that he was later identified only by his clothes, his head being an indistinguishable mass on the ground.

One of the raiders found a carton of candied figs in the mercantile. The raiders, many of them quite drunk by now, found them delicious. When they were brought to Quantrill at the hotel, he had them divided up and given to the ladies gathered there. An extra portion to Miss Rebecca Wheelright who, at Quantrill's request, was playing popular airs on the piano.

Mina Spears, age 43, was gathering eggs in her chicken coop. She held up to the light what she thought to be a double yolker. In an instant it was gone. She found only egg yolk and bits of shell around a perfectly round hole in the side of the coop.

Abolitionist Preacher Hugh Fisher hid in the cellar under his kitchen. He worked himself into the floor joists and tried not to move, though his leg was trembling so badly he had to wedge it among the cross braces to keep it from drumming against the kitchen floor. Three times Quantrill's men came into the basement with lamps, and all three times they failed to see him amongst the joists. Finally, they set fire to the house. Nearly dead, he crawled out in one of his wife's dresses. When he collapsed, she threw a carpet over him, then piled more of their belongings on him until he passed out and could no longer whimper in pain.

At the gun shop, two men were tied together while the shop was being looted. When the guerillas had taken all they needed, they set the shop on fire and threw the two men back into the burning building. When the two managed to right themselves and struggle out the door, the guerillas laughed and threw them back in. They did this two more times before the men gave up and were burned to death.

Henry Barlow was shot fourteen times and failed to die. His wife threw herself over his body to protect him. One of the guerillas picked her head up by the hair, placed his revolver at the base of Barlow's skull and fired, severing his spinal column and killing him instantly.

By nine o'clock in the morning, the Eldridge Hotel and most of the central business district and a couple score of houses had been torched. The grocery, the mercantile, several saloons, all the gun shops and jewelry stores had been sacked. The guerillas had taken what valuables they had been able to find. More than half of them were drunk. One hundred and fifty men and boys were dead. The guests, taken a short distance from the hotel, were not harmed, and no lady of the town was harmed either.

Alaska, 1904.

Later, warming themselves by the fire, the first of the Kansas idlers said. "I don't really think he was Quantrill, do you?"

"Shouldn't have said he was," the other replied.

Note: Historical material in this story was taken from the books Bloody Dawn *by Thomas Goodrich, Kent State University Press, 1991, and from* Quantrill's War *by Duane Schultz, St. Martin's, 1996. Newspaper quotes from* Bloody Dawn.

Real Stories Of True Crime

Len, 1961

He crouched in the dark, listening to his own heartbeat. There was no other noise. He expected to hear sirens, whistles or a clanging alarm bell, but it was quiet. When he stood up and walked around, it was like nothing he had ever seen before. It was magic, like in the stories. Everything was wonderful and everything was his. He was thirteen.

It was an ordinary store, a dime store. He had been in this store hundreds of times before. He had been there that very afternoon. He guessed he liked to look at the stuff. It was O.K.

But tonight, in the store, alone, everything dark, except for the few pools of light from lamps left on to scare off intruders, it was like a kingdom. He said the word to himself, feeling the light pressure of his lips on the "m." He looked back at the little window he had come in, half expecting it had closed up like a wound. It was still there, still open. He fought the impulse to leave.

He reached to his left. It was a small, gold pen, a ball point with a button you pushed to get the point out. To put it back, you pushed the clip. He put it in his pocket. Then he reached out and took a whole handful. He put them in his pocket, too.

He moved around the whole store, taking what he wanted. There was a cap gun and a model car that he liked. Once before, a man had yelled at him for bouncing one of the rubber balls that looked like baseballs. He picked one up and threw it across the store. Then he picked up the rest and threw them. When he stopped, the only sound was the rubber balls, bouncing. He took glue and paint for his model car. He took a football for his friend, Tony. He took some glasses that magnified things up close, but made them blurry far away.

He crawled to the front of the store and got some of the big paper bags to put his stuff in. While he was there, he got cigarettes of all kinds and a lot of candy. Later, he found a big bag for laundry, so he used that instead.

When he knew he could take anything he wanted, he stopped taking as much. He put some of the pens back, and a big wad of rubber bands, too. He went over to the side of the store where there were women's clothes. He picked up brassieres and thin, slick feeling panties, and he thought about some girls he liked and how they wore these things next to their skin.

He picked up some of the panties and held them. Then he unzipped his pants and held the panties to himself. He already had an erection. When he rubbed himself, it was wonderful. He had to hold on to the shelves to keep himself up. He knew he had come, though he never had before. He held the panties to himself and zipped up his pants.

He stood for a long time in the middle of the store, not taking anything, not doing anything. When he finally picked up his stuff, he knew he didn't need it. He was different now, standing here in the middle of the empty store. He knew he would come back and back and back.

Raymundo, 1978

I hadn't seen him in a couple of years. My father I mean. He'd taken off when I was in high school. Just took off. A couple of years later I saw him in this store. A 7-11. I was doing roofs then, and it was hot, the end of the day, and we stopped for a cool one. And there he was, just standing there, buying some kind of ham sandwich. Just standing there, like he was anyone else. I stood by the potato chips and stared at him. I just stared like I was stupid or like he was some kind of movie star. He wasn't no movie star, though. He was my father, only he was older and fatter. I was in good shape back then, doing roofs.

So the next time I see him, it's at this party. It's a birthday party for my nephew Mikey. He's four, my cousin Tina's kid. She's married to big Mike who manages this market up on the northside. A grocery. So the party's for Mike, Jr.—Mikey. And it's nice. As soon as I walk into the backyard I see there are balloons and those twisted paper things strung from tree to tree and over to the porch where the adults are. In the backyard, there's about a million kids running around, chasing each other and having a good time. I look for Mikey, but I don't find him.

I've got this great baseball set under my arm— plastic bat big as the kid himself, whiffle balls, a couple of gloves so all the kids can play and there's no fighting or anything. It's all wrapped real nice. Mike, big Mike, is in the middle of the yard by the barbecue, cooking hot dogs and hamburgers. The kids are screaming by him like Indians around custard, and he sees me and waves. Then he picks up his beer in salute. I can still see that.

The other adults are over on the porch. "Come on over," they say. "Have a beer." The whole bunch is there, Tina, Joe, Arturo, Patty, Martha, Ben. Only I don't see any of them. What I see is him. I stand there with my beer, not even open yet, and I stare at him. He's just sitting there, drinking a beer, and he's got his arm around my mother, just like a long time. He points to me and laughs. They all laugh. "Don't stand with your mouth open," he tells me. "Pour some beer in it. You're a man now." He gets up and shakes my hand, then hugs me to him. "A beer," he says. "*Familia*."

I don't know how much later it is. A couple of hours. A few beers. There are only a couple of kids left. And they're quiet. Patty's kid has crawled up into her lap and gone to sleep. The voices are low. Lots of people have gone into the house, and you can hear them talking and knocking stuff around. Next to me is the table. There's some chips left, some hamburger a kid started and didn't finish. And hamburger stuff, and everything smells like a new onion. The birthday cake is in the middle of the table, only it's just crumbs, an icing flower and a frosting sticky knife now, like a bomb has gone off in the middle of it. The beer cooler is next to me and sometimes I just reach in and hold my hand in the ice water, feeling it get numb. And I'm just sitting there in the almost dark, a beer in one hand, my other one in the cold water, listening to my mother. I've felt a lot worse.

"Why the fuck you come back?" The words sound far away, but I know I said them. "She's better off without you. We're all better off without you. See, we learned something. We learned we don't need you. We never needed you."

I'm up before he even gets near me. I hope he hits me. I think that. I hope he hits me. He's old and fat, and I'm in good shape. I'm quick. I've already kicked the shit out of better than him. And the palm of his hand comes across the side of my face, just like it always did. It goes cold for a second, then it starts to burn. And then I start. Just like I always did. I start to cry. I'm twenty two fucking years old. And I start to cry. And he hits me again. And I'm crying harder, and I catch the hand across the other side of my face. He's using two hands, slapping me first right, then left.

And the damnedest thing. I remember looking at him there on the porch, his eyes wide, his heels scraping against the concrete like he was running nowhere. And even though there isn't much blood, I know he is going to die. Not much blood at all. But on the front of his shirt, there's birthday cake. And there's no blood on the knife either, just a big frosting flower, pushed all the way back, right up onto my hand. And it's the damnedest thing. And no one's saying a word.

Larry, 1986

It started easy, then it got easier. I never intended it. Not really. It's just not the sort of thing you spend a lot of time thinking about. It's just one of those things that happens. Sometimes they happen to you.

I was hanging out, mostly. I was really waiting for someone who, I had finally figured, wasn't going to show. That was a pisser, but what are you going to do? And that was the whole thing of it, what was I going to do? I started walking. If you walk, something will happen. If you stand still something will happen. It's just faster if you walk.

It was a faggot car, really. A Buick with not all that much up front. The seats were some soft fuzzy cloth, and there was a tape deck with tapes by Kenny G. That was just too cute, Kenny G. Could you imagine that? You drive a Buick, you listen to Kenny G, you leave the keys in the car. You're a dickhead. Really. It's like the test. Give yourself 100.

I mean the real idea of going to see Eddy was to get some decent tunes. Then we'd run it around a bit, see some people, hang out. It had three quarters of a tank. Park it and hitch on home.

I never figured it was worth all that much. That was Eddy. We turned that hunk of shit over in half an hour. Two fifty. Jeez, Louise I said. We could do this forever.

Pretty soon it was the slim jim and slide hammer, in and out in under a minute. A good night we could do a couple grand. Think about that. A couple grand a night. By the time you know I got your car, ten beaners are cutting it into parts. It's a sweet life. I never got my hands dirty. Not once.

Michael, 1992

I don't know. I had this job, working in this place that sold auto parts or something. It was all right. I don't know. I mean I didn't get off on it or anything. Four or five days a week I'd stand behind this counter and get stuff for people—alternators, water pumps, head gaskets, spark plugs—that sort of stuff. Half the time these idiots didn't even know what kinds of cars they had. How are you supposed to deal with some jerk-off who doesn't know whether he's got a three-eighteen or a three-eighty-three? It got me down sometimes. I don't know.

The other half knew too goddamned much. Like I was supposed to know what kind of carburetors Ford used in 1973, or what some kind of fuel pump was supposed to fucking look like. And this guy I worked for was always in my face. Like I owed him my fucking life or something.

Part of my job was to deliver parts to gas stations and mechanics and shit. I don't know. I liked that part all right. I'd zip into some garage somewhere, give this guy his wheel bearings or U-joints, he'd sign the slip of paper or something, and I was out of there and moving down the street. And I didn't have to look at anybody's ugly face if I didn't feel like it. It was O.K.

Anyway, this one day, I didn't go to work. I got up, ate my Frosted Flakes, got dressed, but I didn't go. I just didn't feel like it or something. I don't know.

So, I just goofed, you know? I went to a movie or something. I ate some doughnuts. I don't know. But I ended up in this bar. It was just a bar. A neighborhood bar or something. I had never been there before. I just went in on a whim or something. I don't know.

There was this woman there. She wasn't any sort

of a great looker or anything. She was just a woman, drinking in a bar. And she kept looking at me. Like she was interested or something. I don't know.

And we started talking. About the weather or something. She wasn't doing anything, just drinking. She was kind of old. Thirty or something, and she was married, and they said at the trial that she had kids. A girl and two boys.

Anyway, I ask her if she wants to go for a ride or something, and she says, "What the hell?" What the hell? So we go to this lake that's not that far away. It's a place I used to go and just goof. You know, smoke a little, drink a little.

There's a lot of rocks at this one end of the lake. Big flat rocks where people can go and lay in the sun. And there wasn't anyone there. So I took her over to this part of the lake with the rocks or something. "What the hell?" she says. I know she wants it. What the hell?

The next thing I know, she's all over me. Kissing me, pulling at my clothes. We were right out there on the rocks, right out in the open, but there's no one around. So, it doesn't make any difference.

So we just do it. Right there on the rocks.

And after it's over, I'm looking at her. And she's really not that good looking. You know? I mean her tits kind of sag, and they're wrinkled from having kids or something. And there are these marks across her belly. Stretch marks or something. I don't know. But the worst of it is, she's crying. And she's got that black shit around her eyes, mascara or something, and it's running down her face in big globs.

And it hits me that she's married and got some kind of kids or something, and her old man has some kind of job like mine where people get in his face, and the stale old fucker just takes it. And then she goes out while he's at work and gets fucked on some rock by this lake by this guy she doesn't even know. And then she gets all guilty or something. She doesn't say anything. She just sits there crying. Not a sound. But that mascara keeps streaking her face like a witch or something and her wrinkled old tits keep shaking.

And now I understand that it was like the wrong place or something. I don't know. I mean like I was in this place where I thought I wanted to be, and now that I was there, I didn't want to be there anymore. Somehow it was all wrong. I mean the lake, the rocks, her tits. Me. It was just a bad place. I don't know. And then I picked up this rock. And it wasn't that big. And I hit her. And I hit her again, and then again. And I kept hitting her until I bashed out her brains or something. I don't know.

Skeletons

He was a seventeen-year-old boy driving the skeleton of a school bus. In the summer, teams of ten boys took turns driving the skeletons from Deerborn, Michigan, to Mitchell, Indiana. The busses were skeletons because they were going to be assembled in Mitchell. In Mitchell, the busses would receive bodies, floors, seats, doors and windows. Right now there wasn't even a seat in this bus. He sat on a wooden crate nailed to plywood lashed to the bare frame of the bus. There was no windshield or top to the bus. His bus was eighth in the column of ten.

The sun burned his face, arms and neck, and the wind blew dirt and insects into him. The heat of the unshielded engine kept the wind from cooling him off. His face was badly burned he knew, and he had been stung by a bee or something like it, and the swelling above his brow threatened to close his left eye. There was a coating of grit from the road over every part of him.

Each summer two teams of boys from the high school were chosen by the coaches to drive the busses. A team would make twelve trips, three hundred and ninety two miles from Deerborn to Mitchell. Between trips they would take three days off to rest, then they would board a finished school bus, a new bus bound for Michigan, and ride back to Deerborn and start again. It was a job that every boy in school wanted. They were nominated by coaches because the coaches could swear to their reflexes and driving abilities. He had been chosen because his father owned the drug store in Mitchell and knew people in Rotary and Oddfellows.

Trips began at six in the morning and ended at about nine at night. Barring delays from bad weather or flat tires, they would reach Mitchell before dark. If they did not make it all the way, they had to stop and camp for the night, because the busses had no headlights. And they always stayed together in a convoy. If one stopped, they all stopped. On his first trip they had made it home in one day, driving at what he thought must have been about fifty for the last sixty miles from Indianapolis south. He hoped they would not have to stop on this trip. But the second bus on this trip had been overheating since the Michigan border, and he was sure they would not make it back before dark. He had a knapsack with his toothbrush, some peaches and cheese, and a change of underwear his mother insisted he take.

Two weeks before, one of the busses had a blow-out in northern Indiana. The boy driving it, a good baseball player, had lost control of it, spun it into a ditch where it threw him out and rolled over him. It didn't kill him, but it had broken his pelvis and his leg very badly. It was whispered that they were going to cut the leg off, but his father, who knew all the doctors, thought that was just a rumor started by people who knew no better, people for whom tragedy was as entertaining as television.

Television could never be as entertaining as this. He had seen families stopped for picnics along the road. He had seen a dead cow leaning against a barbed wire fence with the hind legs of a breached calf still jutting out of her. He had seen two funeral processions, and thought that maybe a hundred people had waved at him as they drove past. A convey of Army trucks had passed them, and some of the soldiers had waved. He had seen a fat woman at the side of the road bend over, hike her dress, drop her pants and piss like a broken fire hose. He had seen a house that had burned not long before. He had seen wonderful places—parks and campsites where you could have a picnic. There was a girl he liked in school and he thought that maybe some day they could drive up here and have a picnic that she had cooked. And she would admire him for knowing these wonderful places and later, she would kiss him.

Ahead of him, the boy in the seventh bus had extended his arm, straight down. And he knew that ahead of the seventh bus the sixth was slowing down, and then the fifth and so on. The second bus had overheated once again. He looked at the Bulova on his wrist. It was after four thirty, and they were still well north of Indianapolis. Indianapolis was two and a half hours from Mitchell. If they waited for more than a few minutes for bus two, they would have to stop for the end of the light, camp and begin again in the morning.

He did not want to stop. He was not frightened exactly, but he did not want to stop. Here he was the eighth bus in the caravan, seven ahead, two behind, one of the chosen drivers running from Deerborn to Mitchell. When they stopped, he would be the druggist's boy again. And he did not trust the rest of them. He did not play basketball. He was short and thin, and his coordination was less than average. In Indiana, basketball was life. Six of the drivers were basketball players. The others played football, baseball and ran track.

Though he was a little frightened of them, he admired these boys, especially Sam, who was an all-state guard on the basketball team. He was tall and graceful. He was graceful even shooting free throws, bringing the ball up from between his knees and arcing it toward the basket from a crouch. Girls all loved Sam, and he understood why they did. He couldn't play basketball, but he had been to the state finals in science fair, though no one seemed to care, except his mother and the science teacher.

While bus two cooled down, he went off the road into the corn fields to pee, looking to make sure no one followed him. Then he made his way to the front of the caravan where coach Dunleavy drove the station wagon that held the supplies. All the drivers were gathered around the lowered tailgate of the Ranch Wagon. They were laughing and a couple of them were pushing and shoving each other, swearing and laughing. Several of the drivers were smoking cigarettes right in front of Coach, who, when he saw him, said, "Come September, I see any one of you with one of them filthy butts in his mouth, and you're going to be sitting in the stands with the rest of the girls." Everyone laughed, and coach lit his own Chesterfield. "I ain't joking with you, Ladies."

He hung back a couple of steps away from the rest of the drivers, until Coach looked him square in the eye and asked, "And what do you want?"

"A Coca-Cola, sir."

"Well, come up here and get it. I ain't bringing it to you. I ain't your mommy, though I understand I got me a real pretty face."

The group joined in laughter and someone shoved him by the shoulder. He laughed, too. And then Sam took a Coca-Cola from the cooler in the back of the Ranch Wagon and handed it to him. The glass of the bottle was as cold as the ice it had been sitting on, so he pressed it to the bite above his eye and held it there for a while. And when he pried off the cap and took a long drink, it hurt his teeth. Then he stepped back from the group gathered around coach. He took the earplug for his radio from his pocket, took out the little red transistor radio and tried tuning it in. He had hoped he could listen to the radio as he drove his skeleton bus, but the wind noise and the static made it impossible to hear. So he listened when they stopped.

He found a station from South Bend and it was playing a song he liked, "Lollipop." "I call him Lollipop lollipop, oh lolli lolli lolli, Lollipop." He knew some of the basketball players sniggered about the song, but he did not know why. He thought about the girl he liked and imagined that someday she would like him and call him "Lollipop." He was nodding his head and mouthing the words to the song, and he caught himself and stopped it. None of the other boys had radios, and he was afraid someone would take it away from him. They were new, these tiny shirt pocket radios, and he was the only one he knew who had one.

They did not like him, these other boys. They liked boys who played sports and who were liked by the girls. And the girls did not like him, either. He knew that even the girl he liked did not like him. She liked boys like the others, ones who played sports and laughed easily. He had seen the look she gave Sam, and it made him uncomfortable. He had told this to his mother who had told him that someday she would grow out of it, and she would like boys like him, boys who were smart and had some future ahead of them.

The other boys, she said, had no future. But he understood that was not true. They had a clear future. After school, even before they graduated, they would move on to the quarry and begin cutting limestone or to the bus plant they were driving for. They would marry the cute girls. Some of them would join the army, but they would come back in a couple of years and settle in to the jobs at the quarry or the plant, and they would stay there for the rest of their lives.

Sam turned away from the crowd and bumped into him. Sam started to say "sorry," then stopped himself. Sam looked at him and exhaled cigarette smoke from his nose. "Is that one of those transistor radios?" Sam asked.

He nodded.

"I'd sure like to give a listen to it."

He pulled the little flesh colored plug from his ear, took the red radio from his pocket and handed it to Sam. Sam pushed the earpiece into his ear and then rolled the radio up in his tee shirt sleeve, the opposite sleeve from where he rolled his cigarettes. Sam went off down into the field to pee, nodding his head in time to the music.

Coach blew the whistle three times, the signal that they were ready to get back on the road. He climbed onto his wooden crate, turned the key, pumped the gas pedal hard and let the bus chug to life. Sam walked by, snapping his fingers now. Sam took the earplug from the radio out of his ear, and before he even thought about it, he said to Sam, "That's O.K. You can keep it."

Sam stopped, looked at him, pointed his finger at him like a gun, brought his thumb down sharply, grinned and then winked at him.

They pulled out on to the road, moving south again. He was number eight in the convoy of boys, and he had never been happier.

Oncology

Kenneth was thinking about boots when the pain came back. Specifically, he was thinking about whether or not he needed to go home and change his boots, before he parked the tractor and headed up into the mountain to fish. They were new boots, good ones, that he had intended to last a long time. But he had not yet waterproofed them.

To go home and change boots would add an extra half hour, maybe forty-five minutes, and he needed to be home when Sam got out of school. He didn't want to give up forty-five minutes of fishing, but if he got the new boots wet, as he surely would, they would dry and crack and chafe his feet. You couldn't work in bad boots. It took a long time of hard work to make a hundred dollars, and you couldn't buy a pair of decent boots for less than that.

But the pain came back, and that replaced the worry about the boots in his mind. He shut down the tractor and leaned back and tried to breathe slowly and evenly. He tried shifting position in case it was just gas and would pass, but he knew it wasn't. He took the bottle of Maalox from the pocket of his coat and took a long drink. The Maalox and the slow breathing eased the pain sometimes. Sometimes it didn't.

In the distance he could see the mountain. From here it seemed small and inconsequential. But it took a half hour to drive there, and another half hour to reach the top where the lake was. At the lake it was cool and the air was sharp with the smell of pine. He felt better at the lake, even when the pain came. But the pain took time. He couldn't work while it held him, and he supposed that he wouldn't make it up to the lake now that it had started up again. It was getting worse. It didn't come as often, but the bouts with it were longer and more protracted, and it hurt worse. He leaned back in the cab of the tractor, closed his eyes and concentrated on his breathing.

"Jesus Christ." He came awake to the sound of the screen door slamming. His son stopped and looked at him as he lay on the sofa, surprised. "Don't slam the door," he said.
"Sorry. Are you sick?"
"Just don't slam the door, all right?"
"I'm sorry. I didn't think you were home."
"Isn't the truck out there?"
"Yessir."
"Then I'm home. Don't slam the door. Whether I'm home or not, just don't slam it. Got that?"
"Yessir."
"Good. How was school?"
"Fine. Are you sick?"
"'Fine'? That's it? Just, 'fine'?"
Sam shrugged his shoulders. "I guess. It was school. Like always."
"Did you learn anything? Did you fuck up?"
"Yessir."
"Which?"
"Learned, I guess."
"You guess. You better learn. You want to drive a tractor your whole life?"
"Sounds O.K."
"It's not. Learn something. Don't drive a fucking tractor. You want to go fish for a little bit before dark?"
"O.K."
"O.K.? Jesus Christ. Enthuse a little, will you? It's your life. The only one you're going to get. Try for better than O.K., will you?"

"O.K."

"Son of a bitch. Get me that Maalox over there."

The night was cooling off nicely. He sat on the steps of the tractor shed with Wayne, took a pull off the bourbon and passed it back.

"Those were some good fish," Wayne said.

"Lureen cooked them up nice."

"Sam caught them?"

"A couple. He could a had more only he was off day dreaming. He's at that age where he can't keep his mind on anything he should. I guess he's mostly thinking about what it is girls got inside their pants."

"He's a good boy, but he's a boy, that's all. I suspect you were about the same at that age. I know I was."

"I want him to be better."

"Of course you do. You know, we got to get moving on that last field out there. We can get one more rotation if we get it done this week. Otherwise, it's going to be too late. We're going to run right into frost."

"Yeah, I know. I'm sorry about it."

"I ain't asking for no apology. I'm just saying, is all."

He took the bottle back. "I know. I'm trying to get on it."

"I know you are. You're still sick, ain't you? Should you even be drinking that?"

"It's O.K. Whiskey's better than that damn Maalox, which is the worst stuff you can drink. Ever."

"You got to go to the doctor. Let Lureen call Bill Maddox for you. Hell, we'll pay for it. Think of it as the health insurance I don't provide for you."

"I'm not real anxious to hear what he has to say."

"You think it's that bad?"

"Feels like."

"Then you better go."

"You really think Sam is a good boy? I mean he likes you and Lureen and all."

"Yeah, I'd say he was a good boy. Hell, I known

some that is just bad news. Watching them grow is like watching a train wreck."

Kenneth looked off across the small field that was given over to Lureen's garden, where she grew what she needed for them and for the Farmer's Market on Saturdays. Beyond it, he could see his trailer and the faint shadow of Sam in the window.

"He's doing his homework. Like he should. And he's a natural born fisherman. He can just sense where the fish are. Like you can't see or hear them but you know they're down there, waiting. He's a pretty good boy. He could be a lot of help someday."

"What are you saying, here?"

She heard the truck, laboring up the alley, the chained steel canisters, some empty, others full, knocking together with a nearly musical ring. There were three empties in the bedroom, just behind the doorway, just behind his chair. She began to haul them out, tipping each one slightly and rolling it on it edges into the living room. Even empty they were heavy. The driver would do it, but she made them leave the new tanks in the living room and she always brought the empties out there, too. The drivers were nice enough, she thought, especially Ramon, but she had an odd feeling about having a Mexican see their bedroom.

Roy watched her, his eyes rolling like a dog's. His thin hands fluttered on the arm rests of the chair, and then he brought them up to the plastic tubing that went around his ears and into his nose.

"Don't. Don't you move. I do this every damn week and I'll keep on doing it. I don't need your help."

The hands sank back down, the eyes rolled once then went straight ahead and locked. Once this would have been followed by a few minutes of silence, and then the explosion of filthy words, and, then, more than once, the back of his hand to her face. But now he merely stared ahead, the muscles in his jaw tense, adding new planes to his ruined face.

He would stare ahead all of the morning, at the *Today Show* and *Regis and Kathy Lee*, and later at *The Young and the Restless* and *Guiding Light*, her stories, once, now his, though she assumed that during the hours she was out, working at the card shop, he slept.

She stood off to the side while Ramon wheeled in the new canisters and took out the old. He was polite, nodding, smiling, calling her Miz Powell, and then in a new tone of voice, more gruff and off handed, turned toward him and asked, "Howz it, Mr. Powell?" A thin smile would bend his lips and his head would nod, just barely, and his hand would lift off the arm of the chair in a small, weak salute. Men. A word, not even a thought-out word, but just an automatic word from one to the other, seemed more valuable than all of the conversation a woman would gather and stitch together in a whole week.

On Ramon's shirt there was a square patch, just above the oval one that read "Ramon" that said "Tucson Oxygen." She wanted to know how they got Tucson Oxygen. Wasn't oxygen just air they put in tanks? Besides, Tucson was eighty miles away. Why did they have to have oxygen sent all the way up from Tucson? She supposed something else had to come out. There was more in the air than oxygen, but she couldn't think how they would get it out. She didn't suppose Ramon knew, either. He stood patiently by while she took the bills from her purse. Tucson Oxygen no longer accepted her checks, because the insurance had cut them off. She had bounced three checks.

"The insurance," she said. "The insurance should still be taking care of him."

"Yes," Ramon said. "The insurance. It is a terrible thing." He look genuinely concerned.

When he had gone, she began to dress for work. She left a minute or two earlier, every day, stayed a minute or two longer. Working four hours a day at the card shop, she could make enough money to pay the utilities and the groceries, but just barely. It slowed down the rate at which she depleted the savings account paying for the doctor, the oxygen, the medicine. She had not taken out the new mortgage on the house because it had only been paid off for a little over a year. Soon she would have to file the papers. The money they received would just go back into making mortgage payments again.

Dressed, she took him to the bathroom, where, disconnected from the oxygen, he would sit on the toilet to pee. She would leave him there alone, because she knew that sometimes he cried. "Hurry," she said. "Ruth will be over to sit with you pretty soon."

Kenneth had seen a movie once. About gangsters. The bad gangster made the less bad gangster dig his own grave. The less bad gangster had done it. He had dug his own grave, weeping and begging the bad gangster not to shoot him.

How can that be, he wondered. How can anyone make you dig your own grave when you know that you're going to be killed? He imagined himself as the less bad gangster, leaning back, lighting a cigarette and blowing smoke out his nostrils. "Hell no," he said. "I'm not digging my own grave. What are you going to do about it? Kill me?"

"Well, I'm going to hate to lose you, that's for damned sure. You're good help and a good neighbor."

"I wish you would keep Sam. Just for a while. Let him finish school. Later, I think my folks can take him. It's just that my dad's so sick right now."

"I know," Wayne said. "I wish to hell I could. He's a good boy. But Lureen and I aren't young any more. We couldn't deal with a boy, even one as good as Sam. Neither of us has the patience for it any more. You might have to send him to his Ma."

"No. Casey will not get her hands on this child. She's ruined every other damned thing in my life, but she's not going to ruin my boy. I can't begin to tell what

I was thinking when I married her. And she'll find us in Tucson. I have to go to Tucson. That's where my folks are. That's where the big hospitals are. And if I go there, Casey will find us."

"You don't even know what's wrong, though. You haven't been to the doctor."

"I know."

"I just wish you would go to the doctor."

"I'll see enough doctors in Tucson."

He met Casey twelve years before when they were working for New Mexico Fish and Game. They were field agents, taking counts of the fish populations in various lakes. Casey was just out of college, barely twenty, and he was her assistant. They would spend weeks at the agency, preparing reports, then more weeks out in the field, netting fish, counting, releasing, then moving on, netting and counting more.

He had thought it was the best time of his life, spending his days on the water. Gradually, they had stopped driving back to Albuquerque or to motels in the small towns near the mountain lakes. He had tried to figure where Sam had been conceived—tent or truck, but there was no way to tell. He had known that Casey had not loved him. She had a boyfriend in Albuquerque, but they had been friends, and the nights had been long and boring. Their job was a grand adventure, and they had both felt blessed that it was theirs. When she had told him she was pregnant, he had been surprised when she agreed to marry him. He supposed that it was, in some way, easier for her.

When six months after Sam was born, Casey insisted on going back to work, he saw what lay ahead for him. Within a couple of years, Casey was staying out nights, on this or that field assignment. When she finally moved out, she made only the smallest attempt to take Sam, happy to be free again, back with the old boyfriend.

For six years, she left them alone, except for the

occasional weekend, or birthday or other holiday. Then, having married and settled and had other children, she had filed a suit for reconsideration of custody.

Sandra looked at the clock again. She had five minutes to get out of here, and she had just run a new pair of hose. Calvin Kleins at $12.95 a pair. Joshua was still at the table, stabbing his fork at the remaining fish stick, pushing it through the litter of tater tots on the plate. She had to be out of here and on the way to school in twenty minutes, maybe less. She went to school in the evenings, and sometimes, twice, maybe three times a week, she went out on jobs, where she made two to six hundred dollars a night, enough to pay the rent and keep them fed, which Eddie couldn't have done, even if he had stuck around.

She was working to get her Real Estate Broker's license. Real estate was a good deal in Tucson. People kept coming in and buying houses, getting rich and trading up. Real estate agents made good money if they were good and motivated, and she knew she was both. It would be almost as good as going out on jobs. She thought it was funny, how the two kinds of jobs were alike in some ways. You had to have good people skills. You had to be able to talk with strangers, make them comfortable, make them like you right away. You had to be aggressive and willing to work hard, and you did better if you were attractive and made a good showing. The only thing is that you had to pass an exam to be a real estate broker. She would pass the exam, but she hated doing the math. Didn't these people know there were calculators and computers?

"Joshua, honey, come on. Eat your dinner. Linda is going to be here any minute. I want you to be done. Show her what a big boy you are."

"Are you going to work?"

"I'm going to school."

"You're wearing your dress."

"O.K. After school, I have to go to work. Eat your

dinner, Sweetie. You'll be asleep when I get home." She picked up the phone and hit speed dial.

"Not if Linda lets me stay up real late."

"Linda is not going to let you stay up real late. Damn, she's already on her way. You got to finish your fish, Joshua."

"It's not the kind I like."

"It is the kind you like. Come on. Eat the fish and you can leave the potatoes."

"I'll die." This was new, something he had picked up at preschool along with a couple of colds and head lice.

"You will not die. Eat it."

He stabbed the fish stick with his fork, and poked the impaled fish into his mouth all at once. "I will die and you made me."

"Don't talk with your mouth full. Go to the door and let Linda in."

Linda was a small woman, dark, almost pretty, dressed in Levi's and a tee shirt from Cancun. She bent down and scooped Joshua into her arms and picked him up. "What are you eating Big Boy?" Joshua opened his mouth wide to show her.

"Lovely."

"I tried to call you," Sandra said. "I just ran my last pair of hose. I was hoping you had some."

"Just panty hose, Kiddo."

She wrinkled her nose. "Not part of the dress code. Maybe I can stop at Foley's after class."

"Where are you going, tonight?"

"The Hilton? Doubletree? I don't know. It's on a note on my dresser. I'm getting there at ten. I should be out by 11:00, 11:30. If you don't hear from me by midnight, one o'clock, start to worry."

"Start to worry? Girl, I've been worried, ever since I met you. I can't start now. And I really wish you'd find another line of work. I hate to think of you out there with all those maniacs."

"They're not maniacs. They're just guys. Guys

with time and money. This one's nice. I've met him, he's fine. Older guy. No weird stuff, not too much talk. Goes to sleep like a good boy. I'll be O.K. The number's on the dresser."

Linda shook her head, started to say something then bent down to Joshua, burying her nose in his hair. "You smell good, Kiddo. What do you want to do tonight?"

"Popcorn."

"Popcorn O.K., Mom?"

"I guess. Not too much salt, though, and make sure he gets those teeth brushed. I'll be able to get you that fifty when I get home."

"We're not worried about no stinkin' fifty dollars, are we, Kiddo?" She turned Joshua upside down and held him, laughing, by his ankles.

"Someday I'm not going to worry about fifty stinkin' dollars either, but right now, I got to worry about amortization tables, and how I'm going to get across town in twenty-two minutes." She hiked up her dress, bent down and blew him a kiss. "You mind Linda tonight, and you go right to sleep. I'll pick up something nice for breakfast."

"Doughnuts?"

"I don't know. Maybe doughnuts."

"I want doughnuts," he shrieked as Linda bounced him up and down.

"You should have brought him here. He should be with us. His family."

"He doesn't need to see this. Dad's dying. Maybe me, too."

"You're not dying."

"Maybe I am, maybe I'm not, but he doesn't need to see all of this, and you have more than enough to do with Dad and then, later on with me."

"Kenneth. You are going to get better. They're going to make you better at the hospital. People get well now."

"Yes," he said. "Yes, they do. Sometimes. But first they make you a whole lot sicker. They got to nearly kill you to kill cancer. I don't want Sam to see his father that way."

"It's better he sees you and your father that way than not see you at all."

"If I brought him here, Casey would find him in a New York minute. She has people out looking for us. She has people watching this house. You don't know that the damned phone isn't bugged."

"Kenneth, it's not. And there's no one watching this house."

He pointed his finger, put it up in her face. "You don't know. You don't know what that woman is capable of. I do. She would do anything, hurt anyone, just to get her own damned way. She can't find him with Wayne and Lureen, and I'm going to keep it that way."

She moved away from him, back into the bedroom, feeling Roy's eyes following her. Each day less of him moved. Where had Kenneth gotten the finger in the face? She had never done that, and neither had Roy. He would lash out and clip you one, open-handed, but he would never stick a finger into your face like that. It was just plain rude, and there had not been rudeness in this family. Ever. Though she could not for the life of her remember Kenneth ever asking please, or saying thank you, she knew she had taught him that, taught him better.

She began to dust things that didn't really need to be dusted. She had kept a clean house, always, but now she cleaned constantly, moving from room to room, sometimes cleaning the same room twice in a day just to keep busy, just to avoid sitting down in the living room and watching Roy crumble into the dust of ages. And now her boy, Kenneth. She knew it was wrong, but she tried to think what it was she had done to deserve this. To sit by and watch husband and son, dying in front of her, both of them lost in their pain and helplessness, keeping her away, as though it were some club that they had joined, the club of the dying, with its secret rites and signals, all unknown to her.

It was just like them, both of them. They had shut her out since Kenneth was born, father and a son, bound together by whatever it was that bound fathers to sons, not love surely, because she knew what love was. This was not it. It was like something out of a story, how they were bound to each other by anger and disappointment, small signs of admiration, the ferocity of blood, the desire to go out together and take their separate paths to meet only at the death of some small creature—fish or pheasant, frog or deer—as though they saw in the blood of the innocent, the bitter blood that coursed through their own veins, the blood they would not recognize in the other.

And they sat now in the living room, one in the arm chair, strapped to his metal tanks, his hands and body caught in their small motions, the remnants, she supposed, of the body's try for breath, which it no longer needed with the thin streams of oxygen coming in at each nostril. And the other, on the sofa, flat on his back, covered with the afghan, his feet still in the high topped boots he insisted on wearing every damned day, sticking out from the sofa. She would not abide that— she would not abide shoes on her sofa, no matter that he did have the cancer, because everyone can show some decency, even in his last days.

She touched the figurine of the cat, which Kenneth had bought her when he was eight, twenty-seven years ago. How could years simply pass like that, evaporate into nothing but still cling to knick-knacks and photos like the thin film of dust in the folds of the figurine? Even then he had been hardening, turned away from her by his father, who taught him fishing and hunting, and baseball and, mostly, anger. She wanted to push away that hardness now, make him relent and bring Sam home, before it was too late for him, too. She wanted to ask him if it was the right thing to take the loan she saw on the t.v. for 125% of the value of the house. She knew it was not, and that it did not matter that it wasn't right, because they had to have the money, as much as they could. It was an expensive occupation, dying. More expensive than guns and boats and tools. It was the last and most costly hobby of men.

The important thing, when you're running late, is not to let anyone know you're running late. She had spent an extra twenty minutes after class talking with Art about alternative financing. It wasn't going to be on the test, and she didn't think she needed to know it, at least not now. But Art had insisted. He kept coming closer to her, crowding in, letting her smell the Joop! You get one inch closer and it's going to cost you two hundred and fifty dollars, she wanted to say. Instead, she held her ground, looked him in the eye, let him know this was going nowhere.

That was the worst thing about jobs. It screwed up your personal life. Not that she could ever have any interest in a guy like Art, but still, it got all hooked up together, your feelings for guys and your work, because it wasn't all just work. Not completely. You couldn't take yourself completely out of it. Some part of you had to be into it, or it just wasn't going to work. And there was something about being naked in a strange hotel room, with some man you didn't know watching you while you smoked, which she only did when she went on jobs, or drank, which she always did on jobs. And that first touch, to the breasts, to the leg, that was amazing. Always. Suddenly your skin was tighter than the bark on a tree.

But when some guy showed some interest, then there were problems. Like, you always thought of it as business now. And how is some guy going to feel, if he gets real interested, and you get interested, and some time, some how, he's going to learn just what it is you've done to put the bread on the table. And if you get yourself worked up about doing it with strangers, is that going to go away? Even if you settled down? Are you ever going to be content again, just to be with one man? Saturday nights after pizza and beer? She couldn't imagine, and then she could.

She thought about Eddie. She had loved Eddie, maybe still did. If anyone asked her if she ever loved any man, she could say that she loved Eddie. But no one ever asked. It was like everyone thought that anyone who did what she did could never love anyone. But she had loved Eddie. She thought about him often. Somebody else had him by now. Someone had caught him, held on to him. When he got older, tired of running and lying he had probably knocked someone else up, and that someone else had managed to hang on to him. A couple of years ago, he had sent Joshua some Star Wars stuff for Christmas. It was old, dusty stuff, like it had been in a warehouse for a long time and he had gotten it cheap at a flea market or something. But he had sent it, and she had tried to explain to Joshua who this man was who was sending him presents. That was the last she heard from him.

He sat in the parking lot of the hospital. He had driven down in the morning, leaving when it was just light. Now he was here, and the hospital was huge. He had a ten thirty appointment, and now it was ten twenty. No, later.

He knew this much. They would set him in a chair and inject something into him. It would be poison. A strong, bad poison. But it would not kill him. It would make him very sick, but it would not kill him. That was the idea. The poison was enough to kill the cancer, but it was not enough to kill him. It would take a long time, and there was a chance it would not work. It was a very good chance.

He thought of that movie with Gary Cooper. He had seen it on the afternoon movie just a few days ago. "High Noon." With that song going on in the background, over and over. "Do not forsake me, oh my Darling." That was him. He had been forsaken. First by Casey, now by everyone else. He was all alone, facing the hospital and the poison. No one could go with him, no one could help him. He was supposed to go to room J329. He thought about himself walking the long corridors of the hospital where people were sick. He would be sicker than most of them, but they would not know that. They would think he was just fine.

He thought about getting sicker and sicker. He thought about his father, sitting in that chair, strapped to his tank, barely moving, too sick to eat, his body just eating itself so there was less and less of him each day.

He thought about the hotel around the corner, just two blocks to the north. It was ten stories tall. He had never been in a hotel that tall. Only motels. Two stories, max.

She didn't like afternoon dates. She had to drop Joshua off with Linda, then get dressed in the middle of the day in clothes no one else would wear at this hour, and then make it across town in traffic. She had stopped in the lobby and called his room. Late, ten, no fifteen, minutes, she still had to stop in the lobby restroom, dose herself with the spermicidal foam (a quick, hard ballooning of cold, that went suddenly warm and flat and had to be dabbed away as it began to drip). Then she had to re-tease her hair. "Tease" the hair. She didn't even want to think about that one, redo her makeup and head up to 627.

And when she got there, he was just an awkward farm boy, dressed all wrong in a cheap polo shirt (KMart? Target?) jeans and boots, not cowboy, but work boots, hillbilly boots. He smiled quickly, aware of his bad teeth, then motioned her in. She stood in the door.

"Honey?" she asked. "They told you the price, right?"

"Three hundred," he said.

She nodded. Yes, three hundred. "And I don't do any 'special things' for that."

He nodded then. Understood.

Still she would not come through the door. It felt all wrong, and she would have thought that he was a cop, though no cop would have been stupid enough to dress like a plow hand to try to trap her. She fought down her panic, staying just outside the door in case she needed to run. She thought about kicking off her shoes, but didn't, afraid it would tip him off. "In advance," she said.

His expression did not change. He reached into the front pocket of his jeans and took out a folded over envelope. Unfolding it, he extracted a sheaf of bills. He gave her two hundreds, then started on the twenties.

Now she was really weirded out. She stepped inside and shut the door, her heart pounding now. "Not out there, in front of God and everyone." Immediately, she wished she hadn't said it.

He went on counting out the twenties. "Forty, sixty." His hands trembled slightly as he counted the bills into her hand. "Eighty, three hundred."

She stayed near the door and put the bills into her purse, a small white leather clutch, that looked ridiculous at four in the afternoon. She took three condoms, all linked together in their plastic packets. "And you have to wear these. All the time. For everything." All through the room was the smell of intestinal gas, like someone had been sick. It was like a public restroom in here.

He looked at the condoms and then went to the bedside table and placed them there, carefully. "O.K.," he said. "Would you like some champagne?" he asked.

There was a bottle of Korbel on the dresser and two water glasses, and beyond that a bottle of Maalox. She'd had Dom Perignon once when an older man, a nice "gentleman" had given her two hundred extra to drink two glasses and then pee on him. "No," she said. "Thanks."

"You can have it. I don't really like it. Or something else. I was going to ask them to bring me some beer. Good beer. Budweiser. They have all sorts of things. Get what you want." He nodded toward an open binder next to the phone.

"What did you do, honey? Rob a bank?" Oh Jesus. She just couldn't control her mouth. She wished she could call that one back.

He smiled again then, showing his crooked, yellowing teeth. "I rob a bank every time I write a check," he said, and then he laughed. "My father always said that."

"Is he passed on?"

"Not yet."

"Oh, I'm sorry." Again! Jesus creeping Christ. She just couldn't keep her mouth shut when she should. "I mean, is he sick?"

"Aren't we all? I mean, if you're not being born, you're dying, right? We're all heading for the same place. Right?"

There was something odd about the way he said that. He smiled, but he did not really mean to smile. She thought she should be really afraid now, but she felt more comfortable instead. She moved in closer, then sat on the bed, which was rumpled as if he had been laying there. She looked at the television where there was a fishing show with the sound so low she couldn't make out what was being said. Without thinking, she picked up the remote control and changed the channel.

"I was watching that," he said.

"Oh. I'm sorry. I thought you might like something more . . . stimulating. You want to watch some dirty movies with me?"

"I thought I would be on the bass fishing tour once. I was good. Really good. I thought I had a chance to hit it big there."

"The fishing tour?"

He blushed now. He nodded.

"You're a fisherman?"

"Not professional. I was good enough, though. I should have been on the tour."

"Was?"

He shrugged. "I could be. Let me order you something. You just call, and they bring it right up. What do you want?"

She shook her head. "Maybe some water."

"Do you want that fancy water?"

"No. Tap is fine." She could feel a drip starting from the foam. "I have to use the bathroom. What do you want me to wear?"

"What?"

"When I come out. Dressed? Undies? Naked? What would you like?"

"What do most ask for?"

"It varies. But don't think about that. Ask for what you want. This is your party. What would you like?"

He seemed embarrassed now. "I guess I'd like to watch."

"O.K. I'll be right back. I'll take off my clothes in here. Maybe you can help. Would you like that?"

"Sure." He had the phone in his hand now. "I'll order some water for you and some beer. You want any food or anything? Hamburger? They got good burgers."

There are a million stories in the Naked City, she thought. He wasn't a cop. They had gotten past that all right and he seemed harmless enough. Still, she slipped the money under the insole of her shoe, just in case. He was an odd one. Certainly a talker, but a weird talker. She dried herself and took the terry robe from the hook and back into the other room.

He was sitting on the bed, his hands between his knees. He had turned back to the fishing show on t.v. She went up to him and turned her back. "Help me with the zip?"

"I ordered some room service. They'll be here in a minute."

"I'll slip into the robe when they come. Just get

the zipper for me." He just watched. He did not change his position, or his expression. It was not that he was uninterested, but he wasn't leering, either. Finally, she reached back and did the zipper herself.

"You're pretty," he said as she stepped out of her dress.

"Thanks," she turned away again, unhooked her bra, then turned to face him. She thought he was about to cry. Jesus Lord, she thought. Let's get this over. This is going to go on forever. She walked over and picked up his hand and put it to her breast. "It's O.K. to touch," she said. "That's what it's all about." He moved his rough index finger back and forth over her nipple, slow, gentle, tentative. "There you go," she said. "You like that? I do."

He let his hand fall, tracing a faint line down her ribs, over her belly, over the Caesarian scar and let it rest on the band of her underwear. She found the roughness of his hands odd, but not unappealing. "Pull down my panties," she said, trying to be forceful, trying to find what it was he wanted. He took both hands then and pulled them down, holding them while she stepped out of them. He ran his hand over the satin of her garter belt, down to the prickly stubble of her pubic hair, then pulled her to him and held his face to her belly. "You smell nice," he said.

"You want to take off your clothes, or do you want me to?"

"I can."

She sat on the edge of the bed while he undressed slowly. His body was fat, but powerful, and his arms, neck and face were burned by the sun, but the rest of him was fish belly white. He was semi-erect now. He smelled sweaty, but worse, like the sweat of worry and stress, not the good clean sweat of work or exercise. Maybe they could climb into the shower. She wanted to find a way to get him moving and get her home. She moved close, touching his body with her breast and thigh. She took his penis in her hand and caressed it slowly, raking one fingernail lightly across his scrotum. He closed his eyes, let out a long, slow breath, rank with the smell of his bad teeth, and he continued to harden.

Almost as soon as she had the condom on him, he pushed her back on to the bed and pushed into her. "Yes," she said as he labored. "That's it. Come on. Give it to me." But he just labored on, his weight and breath oppressive, the rhythm of his hips unrelenting. She raked his back and buttocks lightly with her nails, then harder, and still he went on, like a wheezing, sweating metronome. He was like a runner just pushing, pushing, trying to make it to the end. He grimaced and slowed. She thought for a second he would come, and then she saw, no. She could hear the rumblings from his bowels, smell the stink of him.

"How old's your baby?" he asked, suddenly.

"What? Four."

"Boy or girl?"

"Boy."

"Are you a good mom?"

"Come on, honey. This is no time to talk about that."

"I'm sick," he said.

"Do you need to go to the bathroom?"

"No. I mean sick. Bad sick."

She stiffened then.

"It's not catching. You can't get it. I'm clean."

She pushed up on his shoulders and rolled away as he let her.

"No," he said. "It's all right. I wouldn't do anything to make you sick. I'm not that kind of fellow. It's cancer."

She thought then she would throw up. "I'm sorry," she said. "I have to go. The time's up."

"I don't want my money back."

"I'm not giving it back. Look, you can have a hand job if you want, but I've got to go."

He began to cry then. "I'm supposed to be having radiation at the hospital. I don't have any money of my own. My mother and father gave me this so I could have treatment at the hospital, but I can't do it. I know what they do to you at those hospitals. My father is dying and this money should be going to his oxygen. I never had anything nice in my life, except for Casey and Sam, and she left me for that engineer. I shouldn't be doing this, I know. I left my boy with friends, like he was some kind of dog or something. But this is all I have left of my life. Please," he said. "Please, I know I'm wrong." He was crying loud, racking sobs, having trouble catching his breath in between them.

She felt her skin start to crawl, and she wanted to be home with Joshua.

"Will you hit me?" he asked. "Hard? With a belt?"

"No," she said. "No specials."

Face The Music

He wants a cigarette. That's impossible. He can't remember how long it has been since you could smoke on an airplane, but it's at least as long as he has been off the cigarettes. Still, he feels the need powerfully, more than he has in years.

He's working on his second scotch, getting ready to catch the flight attendant's eye for another. (How long has it been that stewardesses became flight attendants? Longer than since they banned smoking.) He thumbs through the seat pocket in front of him. He's already looked at the magazine, tried and failed at the crossword puzzle. He looks at the airport maps and reads the music selections. There is no audio on this flight, but he is headed home to face the music.

He's thought of it that way all day long. All day his discomfort has grown incrementally as the time neared to climb on the plane and fly home. By the time he had cancelled his appointments, checked out of his hotel, returned the rental car and made it to the airport, his initial panic had settled into a steady drum of dread that kept time with his own heartbeat.

Looking back, it has all the elements of an accident. He has not intended any of this. It was as if he was driving and let his attention flag for just a bit. The phone rings, she rolls over and picks it up. "Hello?" A chill passes through him like a wave of icy water.

He's fourteen. Out behind the house, he pulls the wilted pack of cigarettes from inside the woodpile where he keeps it hidden. He's careful. He knows there is no one around. He lights the cigarette and takes a deep pull, feeling the smoke curl through his lungs, finding all those small, hidden spots.

He walks around the back of the garage, not more than three steps and comes face to face with his father. The wave of panic crashes over him. There is nowhere to ditch the cigarette, no way to hide it from his father. Inexplicably, he lifts it to his mouth. His father's expression is a curious one, halfway between surprise and amusement. The smoke is still in his mouth, not yet moving down toward his lungs when his father's hand hits, snapping his head to the side, sending the cigarette flying into the wall of the garage.

Neither of them is fully awake when the phone rings. Neither really understands what is happening or where they are. It is the most natural thing in the world. A reflex more than an act. She rolls over, picks up the phone and says, "Hello?" And even as she says the word, he feels himself come around the corner of the garage, coming face to face with his own dread.

"What's that you've got?" His mother's words spin him around. He turns his back to her, hunching over to protect himself and his prize. He's barely had time to touch it, no time to play with it, to feel it race across the floor. It's a stamped tin rat, painted gray, realistic and evil looking. Under the metal body is a set of tiny rubber wheels attached to a friction motor and gears. It has a long black, rubber tail.

He sees it on the store shelf. It's like nothing he has ever seen before. His hand goes to it, touches the cool, smooth, painted metal. He doesn't ask. It doesn't even occur to him to ask for it. It is a simple, natural response. His hand simply closes around it.

"Where did you get that?" His mother asks. Her strong hands pry it out of his fingers. "This is horrible," she says. He's fighting back tears, now, his fingers alternately clenching and unclenching. "A rat," she says.

"This is what you want so bad that you won't even ask? This is what you will be a nasty little thief for?"

He shifts his weight from foot to foot, faster and faster, doing a four-year-old's dance to injustice.

"Nasty," his mother says. "This is so nasty." In the middle of the sidewalk, with people watching—grown up ladies smiling at him, his anger and shame wells up, burning his face and eyes until he can't stand it any more. Once he starts to scream, he can't stop.

"Yes?" she says. She's the older flight attendant, no beauty, but she has a fine, kind face, smiling down at him. He points to his plastic glass, now filled with ice only. She arches a brow as if questioning, perhaps acknowledging, how much he has already had to drink. Then she smiles and nods in understanding and is gone.

"Your mother found this," his father says, holding up the thin square of foil. "She wasn't snooping. She just found it." He nods in acceptance. His father's face is serious, though not grim. He understands already that he's not going to be punished, but he will have to stand up to his father's disappointment and disapproval. What resolve he has crumbles inside of him.

"Are you using them?" his father asks. He shakes his head no, feeling a mixture of relief and shame.

"No," his father says, patiently, as if weighing this in his mind. "Do you need to use them?" Again, he shakes his head, no.

"All right, then," his father says, looking at him to see if he is telling the truth. "You're thinking ahead then. That's good. That's good. I can get you out of a lot of trouble. But there's other trouble I can't help you with all that much. Some trouble you just have to face on your own. You don't understand that, yet. But if you get Sandy or some other girl in trouble, I won't be much help to you. You'll be on your own in a way you've never been before." He reaches out and touches his shoulder. "Be careful." Then he repeats it. "Be careful," as he presses the rubber into his palm. "Be careful where you keep those, too. You've upset your mother."

"Four dollars." Sets the little bottle down in front of him, picks up the empty, and takes his money. "Tough day?" He nods, and she gives him a kind smile.

He's not even especially attracted to her, nor she to him. They meet in the restaurant at the Holiday Inn, finishing up dinner, drinking coffee. They gravitate toward each other, exchanging glances, smiles, finally coming together at the bar for an after dinner drink. He's been on the road twelve days of the last three weeks, three so far just this week. She's been out longer. She rolls her eyes. Three different Holiday Inns, the same floral print chair, two full-sized beds, HBO.

On the sofa in her living room, lying at an odd angle, his shoulder bunched against the back of the sofa, most of her weight on top of him, the muscle over his shoulder blade starts to cramp. But he can't tell her, can't move her or pull her back into reality. He's never been this far before. Unsure exactly how it has happened, he is unsure how to keep it going or how to start again. He's afraid that anything he does or says may make her stop him.

Her blouse is on the floor along with her brassiere. Her jeans are bunched around her knees. He keeps moving his right hand up and down her bare back. His left hand is inside her underpants, and he is trying to move them past her hips. His own jeans and underpants are pulled halfway down his hips. Her hand is on his penis, squeezing, hard. He keeps his mouth on hers, swallowing her little moans. "It is going to happen," he thinks. "This is it," just as the lights go on.

"Jesus Christ." Her hair covers his face, but he sees her father standing there framed by the door. And suddenly she is up, off the sofa, struggling with her jeans, scrambling for her blouse and brassiere, and he is exposed and scared as her father comes toward them, his face an index of rage. He's still struggling with his jeans when her father grabs her arm, spins her out of the way and pulls him off the sofa by the front of his unbuttoned shirt.

"Get out of here. Get the hell out of here." Sandy is against the living room wall, sobbing, trying to get her blouse buttoned. He's in front of the door, jeans up, but unbuttoned, shirt open and torn. He opens the door, and he runs.

In his car, on the way home, Peter and Gordon are singing about a world without love. He pulls over, takes the cigarettes from the glove compartment and tries to light one, his hands shaking hard. Suddenly, he is sitting at the side of the road, lit cigarette hanging out of the side of his mouth, sixteen years old and sobbing like a baby, afraid, and ashamed of his own fear and cowardice. Sandy, half-dressed, crouched by the wall while he ran.

They have just finished, been sleeping, dozing, only a few minutes when the phone rings. It is all strange and unfamiliar to both of them. She, knowing only that she is in another Holiday Inn, rolls over and answers the phone. In the few seconds it takes her to pick up the phone and say, "hello," he knows, instinctively that it is his wife. "What?" she asks. "Who?" Then she rolls over and hands him the phone, her eyebrows already rising in apology.

"When your father gets home," his mother says, "he's going to be mad." He's sitting in his room, on the bed, thumbing through a copy of *Boy's Life* that he can't force himself to read. The words won't stay still on the page.

"It was an accident," he says. Though he knows it wasn't, it was something like one. He can't believe it happened. He picked up the rock from the side of the road as he and Bruce walked home from school. He just held it in his hand for a couple of blocks, occasionally tossing it in the air and catching it.

"Think I can hit that little kid up there?" he asked Bruce. The kid was at least fifty yards ahead of them.

"Not with an elephant gun," Bruce said.

He threw the rock more up than out, not really aiming it even, just trying to get some distance on it. It

~153

arced up beautifully, passed its zenith and began its descent, getting more and more frighteningly close to the little kid as it came down.

The kid was screaming by the time they got there, and there was more blood than either of them had seen before. He and Bruce kept watching each other, fighting the impulse to run.

"It was an accident," he repeats.

"We'll see about accidents," his mother says. "You tried to hurt that little boy. You did that intentionally. What kind of person are you? You just sit there and wait. You're going to have to face the music this time."

"Drink up," she says, softly. "We're landing in just a minute."

He drains the glass and hands it to her in exchange for another of the kind smiles. With nothing in his hands, with nothing to do, he sits and waits. The pressure of descent has plugged his ears and released. He waits for the jolt of landing.